HOW TO SURVIVE WITHOUT GROWN-UPS

Mum and Dad

Me

LARRY HAYES

ILLUSTRATED BY KATIE ABEY

SIMON & SCHUSTER

First published in Great Britain in 2021 by Simon & Schuster UK Ltd

1 3 5 7 9 10 8 6 4 2

Simon & Schuster UK Ltd
1st Floor, 222 Gray's Inn Road
London
WC1X 8HB

www.simonandschuster.co.uk
www.simonandschuster.com.au
www.simonandschuster.co.in

Simon & Schuster Australia, Sydney
Simon & Schuster India, New Delhi

A CIP catalogue record for this book is available
from the British Library.

PB ISBN 978-1-4711-9834-2
eBook ISBN 978-1-4711-9835-9
eAudio ISBN 978-1-3985-0007-5

Printed and bound by CPI Group (UK) Ltd, Croydon, CR0 4YY

FSC
MIX
Paper from
responsible sources
www.fsc.org   FSC® C020471

*For Eliza and Johnnie, thank you
for letting me borrow your names*

THE YEAR 2053
FIVE DAYS AFTER
OUR WORLD ENDED

It's Day 5 and things are bad.

You're probably wondering what I'm doing here.

My name is Eliza; I'm the one stuck in the car.

The car is floating in space, a million miles from Earth. It's weird, but the radio's still working and I can hear 'Life on Mars?' singing out from one of the speakers.

My baby brother, Johnnie, has got it worse – he's trapped in the boot with our dog and a bomb. And from his high-pitched shriek I can tell he's just spilled his milk on a dehydrated vampire squid that's about to rehydrate and suck away their faces.

1. LOW AIR

2. REHYDRATING SQUID

3. BOMB

You're probably worried about us. You're probably holding your breath, thinking, *What happens when the air runs out?*

But don't worry – never worry, ever. There's no point. I learned this the hard way five days ago.

HOW NOT TO WORRY (THE HARD WAY)

I used to worry all the time. About everything.

Life for a kid in the year 2053 is tough. We've got all the old problems that kids have always had to worry about, and then a whole load more NEW problems. In 2053 there's absolutely nowhere to hide.

Teachers can even see what you're *thinking*.

Bullies can bully you *anytime*, *any*where.

Sadie Snickpick (AKA the Butt-Flush Bully) can hack into anything. Even the school's 'smart' toilet, and can flush it whenever she wants.

Then there's all the normal stuff that kids have always worried about.

Like, will I die in PE?

MR MURRAY, MY EVIL PE TEACHER, IS TRYING TO KILL ME.

And: is my little brother cleverer than me?

GENIUS LITTLE BROTHER

It all adds up to a big fat worry nightmare.

Mum says I've just got a big imagination. You'd think that was a good thing, but I'm a bit *too* good at imagining a catastrophe. She also says I need to think less. Which is, like, the worst advice anyone has ever given anyone.[1]

---

1 *Don't* believe me? Then don't think of your teacher sitting on this toilet. See, told you.

It never used to be like this. Everything used to be perfect. So I know exactly how bad things have got now.

We live in an old windmill on a cliff that is being eaten by the sea. It makes us the Weird Family but kind of cool at the same time. We have a slide into the sea (which is pretty impressive, but Mum's the only one brave enough to use it) and we have our own beach with a coral reef (Dad built it when our swing fell over the cliff[2]).

And, once upon a time, my parents were the best parents in the world.

My dad's an inventor; he's got a workshop and everything. He works for a massive company called **No Ahhh Technology**© who do lots of high-tech, ground-breaking, science-y things. And when he was still just a schoolkid, he invented the BIN.

---

2   Don't ask me how he did it. He spent months tying little bits of coral to the sunken swing and they just kind of grew.

No, not a rubbish bin. A **BIN**. A **B**rain **I**nterface **N**ode.

An amazing bin.

An amazing BIN that's basically a thing you stick in the back of your head that allows your brain to connect to a computer.

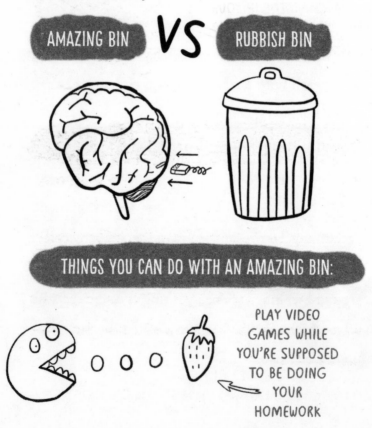

AMAZING BIN **VS** RUBBISH BIN

THINGS YOU CAN DO WITH AN AMAZING BIN:

PLAY VIDEO GAMES WHILE YOU'RE SUPPOSED TO BE DOING YOUR HOMEWORK

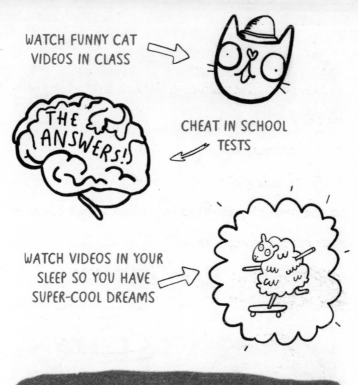

WATCH FUNNY CAT VIDEOS IN CLASS

THE ANSWERS!!

CHEAT IN SCHOOL TESTS

WATCH VIDEOS IN YOUR SLEEP SO YOU HAVE SUPER-COOL DREAMS

THINGS YOU CAN DO WITH A RUBBISH BIN:

PUT RUBBISH IN IT

Genius, right? Maybe even billion-dollar genius?

It could have been, except everyone got terrified we'd turn into cyborgs, so **BIN**s were banned all over the world back in 2029. My dad made precisely £zero.

THIS IS HOW MUCH MONEY MY DAD MADE FOR INVENTING THE AMAZING BIN

DIDDLY
SQUAT
Zilch

THIS IS HOW MUCH MONEY SOMEONE ELSE MADE FOR INVENTING THE RUBBISH BIN

You'd think he'd be gutted, but Dad never seems upset about anything. He's always too busy inventing stuff. And, besides, he's also invented the world's funniest joke.[3]

And when I was small Dad used to invent the best games ever, mainly using our old brown sofa as a pirate ship.

Then there's Mum. Mum's an astronaut who

 hasn't been into space yet. Which doesn't make sense, but she calls herself an astronaut and nobody says 'Aren't you a *trainee* astronaut until you actually go up?' because that might hurt her feelings.

---

3 It's true. I've got it safe in a stuck-down envelope.

World's Funniest Joke. WARNING: THIS JOKE IS SO FUNNY IT COULD KILL. ONLY OPEN IN AN EMERGENCY!

I mean, she finished the astronaut-training programme and everything. And she got a job on the space programme, at the company where Dad works, so she's on a waiting list for her first space flight.

When I was small there were never any rules (apart from one) and Mum and Dad always wanted to play with me. Always.

THE WEIRD FAMILY – HOUSE RULES

Rule no. 1:
If you want to pick your
nose and eat it do it in
your bedroom.

Rule no. 2:

Rule no. 3:

Rule no. 4:

They were great, and they thought *I* was great.

I wasn't afraid of anything back then. I had no idea that I had everything to lose. Then my brother was born. And I lost everything.

That was five years ago. And **TWO THINGS** soon became obvious.

THING NUMBER 1: Johnnie's a genius, just like Mum and Dad. But maybe even more. Mum ate loads of sardine sandwiches when she was pregnant with him, and the doctors said the fish oils made his brain surface go extra-foldy.

I'm sure if you smoothed out the surface of Johnnie's brain it would cover an area the size of a basketball court.

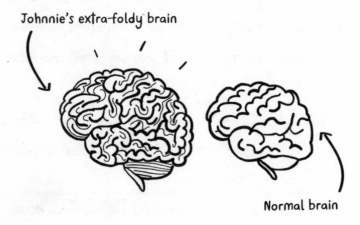

Johnnie's extra-foldy brain

Normal brain

When he was born, Johnnie was so clever he didn't even cry. He spoke. An actual word.[4]

Having a genius baby brother is (obviously) the worst thing ever. You wouldn't like it either, trust me. No one would. For a start, he's better than me

---

4 I know you don't believe me. But it's 100%, **IN BOLD**, <u>DOUBLE UNDERLINED</u>, SIZE 18 ***TRUE***. Mum always said it was just a burp, but I *know* – I was there.

at everything. And I mean *everything*: maths, music, science . . . everything. If I write a story, Johnnie writes a novel. I make up a song? Johnnie will compose a symphony. Anything I do, Johnnie's there, just waiting to outdo me. I swear if I invented something, Johnnie would go out and win the Nobel Prize.

But that's not even the worst of it. There's the **second thing** about Johnnie that makes things so much worse. Oh so much worse.

THING NUMBER 2: Johnnie has a weak left leg.

So what? That doesn't sound too bad, you're probably thinking. But the doctors are worried. And Mum and Dad are worried. **Dead** worried. His weak leg is probably going to turn into something worse. One day, he might stop being able to walk, and he might even never get to be a grown-up. When I play with Johnnie, I sometimes think about that, and it makes me want to cry.

Right now, Johnnie's weak leg isn't a huge problem. If he runs, he sometimes veers off to the left. And he struggles a bit on stairs. But Johnnie is a genius, and things that would totally frustrate you or me don't hold him back for a second. Not one.

Brain = strong

Left leg = weak

The worst thing is not knowing what will happen next. Most doctors say he'll get weaker and weaker. Mum and Dad say we've got to be hopeful, but the hope – the waiting, the not knowing – is killing our family.

The hope means my parents work all the time now for **No Ahhh Technology** © and it's miles away and we don't see them all week. Dad works for *zero* money. Instead he gets funding for inventing a cure

16

for Johnnie, and Mum's working super hard earning *extra* money so we can live in the meantime.

I only really get to see them on Sundays. The rest of the time Gran looks after us. Her idea of childcare is to look disappointed and tell me to be more like Johnnie.

GRAN IS TOXIC

No one likes a cry-baby!!

Look at Johnnie. He makes his own breakfast.

Just think before you go running to Mummy – she has enough problems!

Why can't you just be EASIER, Eliza?

Even when they are around, Dad mainly plays pirates with Johnnie because he feels guilty. He thinks I'm too old for pirates now, so Johnnie and Dad play on the old brown sofa that used to be *my* pirate ship, and I'm lucky if I get tied up and fed to sharks.

Mum feels guilty too, and she really hates seeing me unhappy. So she's always trying to solve my problems because she knows I'm useless and can't solve them myself. But the truth is they can't be solved, unless I can feed my PE teacher, Mrs Crosse and Sadie Snickpick to real sharks.

But then, just under a week ago, the day after my tenth birthday, the day I now call Day Zero, my disaster zone of a life went nuclear.

DAY ZERO: THE DAY MY WORLD ENDED

It all came out of the blue.

We were playing in the garden when Mum and Dad called us in. Mum's a hugger; she'd normally grab me and say something lame like, 'I've been missing you,' even though I'd only seen her ten minutes before. But this time she just looked blank. Blank and weird like she was staring at her phone. But without the phone. Dad looked blank too, which is slightly more normal, but that's only if you've caught him before his first coffee.

They sat us down and Mum said, 'We've got some news.'

I was immediately *on edge*. If your parents ever

tell you they've 'got some news', trust me, it's gonna be really bad.

WHAT PARENTS SAY AND WHAT THEY MEAN

'We've got some great news' = We're going out and the weird boy from next door is babysitting.

'We've got some good news'= We're going to visit the local history museum.

'We've got some news'= Your hamster's died (again).

With parents you have to translate *everything*.

They both smiled, and Dad said, 'We love you very much, but . . .'

I was immediately *terrified*. Nothing good comes

after that, ever. Dad had a sad face. This was going to be truly awful.

'We're leaving home.'

I was immediately *relieved*. This was just one of Dad's jokes. My dad loves 'zany' jokes; they don't even have to be funny.

Johnnie and I waited patiently.

The punchline was coming.

We just had to sit this out.

'Our boss, Mr Noah, has offered us the Chance of a Lifetime,' Dad continued. His eyes looked dangerously bright. He turned to Mum, and together they said in one big happy voice, 'We're going to be the first people on Mars.'

Johnnie's chin and lip started trembling. If this was a joke, Dad was taking it to another level.

Then Johnnie started crying. Proper crying. I gave him a squeeze.

'It's just a joke, Johnnie.'

I glared at Mum. It was time to end this. She shifted about on her chair. They both looked so weird, I was *sure* the punchline was coming. But all they said was:

We're so sorry. There's no room on the rocket.

You can keep the dog.

Mum looks like she's desperate for a wee

Dad looks like he's in the middle of one

And finally: 'We're leaving home tonight.'

And finally-finally: 'Why are you crying? I know it seems like the worst thing ever now, but this is what children dream about! TOTAL FREEDOM. Freedom to do anything you want. Go to school, don't go to school. Pick your nose. Eat it. Flick it. Kill ants. Look at a screen all night.'

I said, 'Dad, please don't go away.' And then I cried.

Myrt jumped on my lap, like she always does, but Mum just stared at me. No hugs, not even a smile. Dad looked confused, like he was struggling with a fart. For a moment I thought he was going to burst out laughing, but then he shook his head and gave me a pat on the arm.

I remember thinking, *A pat on the arm? What sort of parent gives their kid a pat on the arm?* I'd spent years being suffocated by hugs and cuddles from both of them, and now all I got was a pat on the arm.

'Sorry, Elizaroo,' he said, 'but this is the Chance of a Lifetime.'

It was all so weird that my brain struggled to

catch up with itself. I remember Johnnie asking, 'When will you come back?' And I remember holding my breath and then I remember Mum smiling and saying, 'We're not coming back; there's only enough fuel to go one way.'

I ran up to my bedroom and cried until the snot came out. And then I sucked it over my top lip and down into my mouth until I felt sick. Then I vommed it all up in the bathroom, and the whole cycle started over again.

Until I fell asleep.

HOW TO SURVIVE WITHOUT PARENTS

When I woke up on Day 1 of my new life, I kept my eyes shut for the longest time. I figured nothing bad could happen until I opened them. And if I just waited long enough, maybe it would all turn out to be a crazy dream.

But deep down I knew this was real. I went through to the kitchen, and there was no Mum, no Dad, just Johnnie, sleeping in the dog's bed with the dog. I suddenly realized that I'd left him to say goodbye to Mum and Dad all on his own. And now I didn't know what I'd say to him when he woke up.

There was an envelope on the table with my name on it – *Eliza Lemon* written out in Dad's neat old-fashioned handwriting.

I just stared, too afraid to open it.

Johnnie finally woke and yawned his way to the table. He struggled up on to his chair. 'What's that?' he eventually asked, looking at the envelope in my hand.

'I don't know. It's from Dad.'

He took the envelope, ripped it open and read.

Morning, Eliza,

Welcome to the first day of your new life! The good news is that there's nothing left to worry about. The worst thing that can ever happen to you has happened.

Sorry we had to leave home, but this is the Chance of a Lifetime. And remember: anything's possible, but only if you can stop worrying all the time. You knew that when you were small, but you've somehow forgotten it.

Tell Johnnie we love him too. Good luck!

Lots of love and kisses,

Daddy (and Mummy) x x x

PS Call Gran if you need anything.

Johnnie's chin was twitching; he was gonna cry.

'Do you think that's true?' he asked. 'Is anything possible if you can stop worrying?'

'Don't be stupid – of course not.'

I took the letter and read it twice. Dad was mad if he thought we'd call Gran for help. She'd get rid of Myrt in a heartbeat, just because Myrt bites her every now and again.[5] I'd rather be adopted. But Dad was right about one thing: there *was* nothing left to worry about. The worst thing ever *had* happened.

I sat there, rereading the letter, and after all these years full of worry, I just felt empty. Like I'd puked up my brain with all that sick. Sure, there were still loads of things that could get worse, but when I

---

5   **Myrt is (a bit) Savage.**

Don't think badly of Myrt. She just gets (a bit) angry now and again. And she *hates* Gran's orange cardigan. It's a long story, but, don't worry, I'll explain it all later on.

tried to think about what else might go wrong, for once, I just . . . couldn't. For the first time in my life my imagination stopped working.

'Breakfast?' asked Johnnie, getting up from the table.

One of the things I don't get about Johnnie is that he can be totally upset one second, and I mean totally, totally upset, but completely fine the next. That was what happened now. He just climbed down from the table and asked if I wanted scrambled eggs.

And the next moment he was standing on a chair, scrambling away at the hob. He was smiling to himself, and suddenly I felt a rush of anger.

'How can you stand there making eggs? Mum and Dad have left us, and they're NOT COMING BACK. Do you understand? They're NOT COMING BACK.'

I immediately felt bad. This was the pattern of

my life: always doing stuff that I regretted. Johnnie looked sad again and stabbed at the pan with his spatula.

'Don't worry, 'Liza,' he said. 'We'll think of something.'

I knew he was actually thinking, *Don't worry, I'll think of something*. But before I could force him to admit it, the eggs were ready. So we sat at the kitchen table and ate them.

'I've been reading up on how to survive without parents,' he said through a mouthful of egg. 'There's a chapter in *The Book of Secrets*.'

He waved the book at me before opening it. *The Book of Secrets*. It was his most treasured possession in the whole world, and I was immediately interested.

'It doesn't look *that* hard to be honest. There's even a chapter on how to become a kid millionaire.'

I looked blank, so he just kept talking.

THE BOOK
OF SECRETS
A BAJILLION
THINGS GROWN-UPS
DON'T WANT YOU
TO KNOW

If you don't have a
copy, get one. It's
the best book ever
written.
I have to steal
Johnnie's when he's
not looking.

'You know, so we can hire servants to do everything that Mum and Dad did for free.'

Another few minutes and Johnnie would have been well on his way to becoming a billionaire. But before he could start reading, a single word changed everything.

It was me who spotted it. One word written on

the back of Dad's letter. If the letter itself was weird, then the back was Super Weird. So Super Weird it made my heart shiver.

The writing looked like a toddler's, or maybe someone using the wrong hand, maybe even their foot. And there really was just one word . . .

HELP

My hands were shaking as I put the letter back down on the table. Did Dad write that?

'You need to call them,' said Johnnie. 'Use your new phone.'

I tried Mum first, but it cut straight to voicemail. Dad's just rang and rang and then went dead.

I looked at Johnnie. 'So what now?'

'I dunno. We could see if there's anything on the news?'

So we did. And there was. And the news was bad.

THE NEWS WAS BAD

Three rockets filled the screen. They sat on a launch pad surrounded by rainforest. Nothing much was happening, but the whole thing looked like a giant movie set.

In the background, sticking out above the trees, was a giant pyramid. Like an ancient ruin in the jungle, except this one looked brand new and made of metal. We saw text scrolling across the bottom of the screen that said stuff like, 'Mars Mission is GO' and 'Astronauts make the Ultimate Sacrifice'.

But the bad bit, the truly awful bit, was the timer, ticking down at the bottom of the screen like a countdown of doom.

'They're going in two days!' said Johnnie, as if I was too dim to work it out myself.

Two days. We had two days to save our family.

I looked at Johnnie, but he was transfixed by the TV. And when I looked up, I could see why. We were back in the studio and the newsreader was looking up at a huge screen. And there, sized like giants, were Mum and Dad. They were sweaty and smiling. Johnnie hit the volume button and Dad's voice came booming out.

'We're just so proud. This really is the Chance of a Lifetime.'

That weird phrase again. Then Mum was talking.

'We just can't thank Mr Noah enough. Without his vision, his ambition and his money, this was just a wild dream.'

The camera panned upwards and we saw a man floating about in the sky above them, suspended beneath a giant balloon.

'Is that Mr Noah in a personal levitation device?' asked the newsreader.

I turned to Johnnie and asked, 'Who's Mr Noah?'

He tried to shush me.

'I'm serious. Who is he?'

Johnnie looked at me in disbelief. 'You don't know who Noah is?'

I shook my head.

'As in, the richest man on the planet? The guy who invented the flying taxi?'

I shook my head again. Johnnie was trying to make me feel stupid. And he was doing a good job.

'As in Mum and Dad's boss?'

That's where I'd heard the name! I immediately felt like an idiot for not remembering.

But the newsreader was getting excited. 'Can you tell us anything about your top-secret island's current location?'

Mum looked at Dad, and Dad looked at Mum. Then they turned to the camera and said together, 'Sorry. Mr Noah takes his privacy very seriously.'

And then it was chaos. The man with the balloon came crashing into the camera, knocking it on to its side so that all we could see was a few metres of grass. Then a bearded face leaned over and smiled.

'Sure am sorry abou' that,' it said with a twang.

And then the feed went dead, leaving the presenter looking a bit flushed and stuttering.

'Well, there you have it. Laurence and Sophie Lemon, launching this week in their attempt to be the first people to land on Mars. Destined to live and die on the red planet.'

I hit the OFF button. My head was spinning. None of this made sense. Were they just acting for the TV camera? Did they actually want to go Mars? Did they want help? Why can't parents ever just say what they mean?

Johnnie was smiling; everything seemed obvious to him. 'Eliza, we've got to go and save them.' He pulled a face when he saw my reaction. 'Don't look like that, Eliza. We've got two days.'

'Johnnie, we don't even know where it is. No one does. What part of "*secret* island" don't you understand?'

But Johnnie wasn't listening.

He never listens.

'We've got to try to rescue them.'

He left then, off to his room, climbing the stairs one step at a time. And leaving me with half a plate of scrambled eggs and a fully scrambled brain.

I wanted to cry again. Myrt took one look at me and decided she'd be better off with Johnnie. I followed her to his bedroom and found him knee deep in maps. Dad makes him a new one every time they play pirates.

'They're just for play, idiot,' I said, ready for an argument. 'They're not real.'

Not realizing that would turn out to be the most

idiotic thing I'd say all week.

'You're the idiot.' Johnnie shoved a map at me. 'Look.'

I looked at the map with no idea what I was supposed to be looking for.

'It's a map. So what?'

'Look,' he said again, now smiling. 'What do you see?'

The map was just like all Dad's treasure maps and was written on baking paper with a 2B pencil. It had everything you'd expect from a pirate map: sharks and sea monsters and crosses.

I looked at it but only for a bit. Then I lost my temper.

'So what? It's just a map, like all Dad's other maps.'

'Just look,' said Johnnie for the third time. I really was about to scream at him.

'Look at what?'

PIT OF DESPAIR
OAK TREE
?
GO HERE
HYDROELECTRIC
CLIFFS OF INSANITY
BUTTERFLY CITY
RAI
FIRE SWAMP
CAVES
N
W
E
S

LAUNCH SITE: 48°34'12.2"N, 13°59'26.5"W

'FAREWELL, O SUN!
RETIRE BENEATH
THIS OPEN SEA!'

REAL EASTER ISLAND
STATUES

MANGO SWAMP

FOREST

LOGGERHEADS
HATCHING?

CLASHING ROCKS

LIGHTING SAND

ONLY
WAY
IN!

'IT'S NOT DOWN ON ANY MAP; TRUE PLACES NEVER ARE.'

Finally he pointed.

And it took my breath away.

There, slap-bang in the middle of the island, was a giant pyramid, just like the one we'd seen on TV.

'Do you think the map's real?' I said, holding my breath.

'Yeah,' said Johnnie, tears of excitement filling his eyes. 'There's even a map reference.'

The longitude and latitude meant nothing to me at the time, but Johnnie soon had his atlas out.

'Look, there's nothing there.'

'It is not down on any map,' I could hear Dad's voice during our pirate games, 'true places never are.'

Johnnie pencilled a cross in the solid-blue Atlantic Ocean.

'It's not even that far.'

That was a bit optimistic. It was at least 200 miles away.

'Now we just need to get there.'

Myrt was getting wriggly and I gave her a hug. For the first time I felt a flicker of hope. Followed by a flicker of worry. Why would Dad make us such a detailed map of where he worked?

'So what now?' I asked, and Johnnie pulled out a scrap of paper with a list on it.

A to-do list.

TO-DO LIST

- Locate secret island
- Get survival kit
- Get pirate ship
- Get to secret island
- Rescue Mum and Dad
- Make Mum and Dad want us again

'Johnnie, this list is insane.'

Johnnie ignored me and struck a line through the first item.

'Number one done,' he said with satisfied smile. 'Number two is *Get survival kit*.' He looked at me expectantly.

'I can do that, but what about number three? And number four? Johnnie, this is impossible.'

'Leave three to me. You just get the survival kit.' He gave me his serious face. 'The right kit is everything, yeah?'

We stared at each other for a few long moments, but there was no arguing with him. And he was right about one thing – surviving without parents and surviving an impossible mission would all come down to having the right stuff. The right kit *is* everything. Think about it. Who would win in a fight, a tiger or a puppy with a bulldozer?

And I'd read enough books to know exactly what we needed. So I drew up a second list in my journal:

SURVIVAL KIT

First-aid Kit – must contain bandages (for disguise among flesh-eating mummies/ for rope)

A safety pin (to put the pin back in a hand grenade/pin a ripped coat)

Scissors (to cut the wire on a bomb/give to baddies and hope they run with them)

Balloons (to lift something from the seabed/pretend someone's farting)

Some seeds (to grow food/befriend a bird)

A seven-colour super felt-tip (for emergency colouring, e.g. camouflage)

Packed lunch (obvious)

World's Funniest Joke (obvious)

The Book of Secrets (super obvious)

I found everything on the list, stuffed half in my school rucksack and half in Johnnie's ladybird backpack and met up with him in the kitchen. He was lying on the floor, wearing a head torch and looking at the ceiling through a telescope.

'OK, let's get the pirate ship ready.' He jumped up and started pushing at the brown sofa.

That was when I realized something truly awful. Johnnie wanted to rescue Mum and Dad using the old brown sofa. Johnnie wanted to *pretend-rescue* our parents. When you're five, pretend and real, real and pretend, they're both the same. That's why Johnnie was so cheerful. In Pretend World rescuing our parents was easy.

It was so sad. An undersized five-year-old genius who thought playing pirates was real. Who thought he could save his mum and dad with an old brown sofa.

It was even sadder when Myrt tried to join in. She's tiny, even for a cocker spaniel, and Johnnie's weak leg means he's got the pushing power of a chihuahua.

'Johnnie, what are you doing? This isn't a game.'

He looked at me as if I'd pooed in his end of the bath. 'Would you just help push?'

His eyes were wet. He was going cry again if I didn't do something.

'Eliza, just help. Please.'

If you have a little brother or sister, then you know it's always easier to go along with the pretend stuff. Burst the pretend bubble and you make them crazy-sad. But if Johnnie got stuck in Pretend World now, rescuing Mum and Dad would be impossible. I tried to explain, but in the end I couldn't do it. I couldn't destroy his little pretend world that was keeping him safe. So I gave the sofa a shove, thinking of all the ways we were going to fail.

The sofa had wheels, so it wasn't exactly hard to get it moving. It clattered across the kitchen tiles and then bumped out through the double doors. And then it slid on to the lawn, looking like it would slip across the wet grass, down the slope, over the cliff edge and into the sea. This was getting dangerous.

'Johnnie, this is stupid. There's a million ways this will go wrong.'

The sofa would sink in five seconds. We'd drown. And even if it didn't, the Atlantic was huge. We'd never get to Mum and Dad. And in two days? Even if we did get there in time, what if Mum and Dad 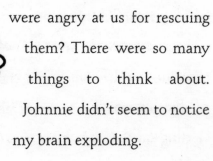were angry at us for rescuing them? There were so many things to think about. Johnnie didn't seem to notice my brain exploding.

'Please stop talking,' he said, climbing on board. 'You can always think of a million ways anything can go wrong.'

'You can't tell me what to do. You're not in charge.'

'Please just stop talking and push. Please?' He looked at me with something between pity and despair, and it made me mad. I gave his pretend pirate ship one almighty get-lost-and-die shove. And immediately regretted it.

It moved slowly at first. Then Myrt jumped on and it picked up momentum. I saw Johnnie's face flip to fear.

'Come on, 'Liza. Get on!'

For a moment I watched, paralysed, as the sofa slid across the lawn. It was about to hit the steep bit, the bit that led all the way to the slide off the cliff. Getting on that sofa meant certain death. But the alternative was worse: if I stayed here, he'd be alone.

And so would I.

I ran.

I jumped, and Myrt and Johnnie dragged me aboard just in time. We had about eight seconds to enjoy the ride before we hit the slide and rode it over the cliff. Over and down into the Atlantic Ocean.

'Johnnie!! We're gonnaahhhhhhhhhh,' I screamed all the way down. And then we hit the water with a horrible bone-juggling SMACK.

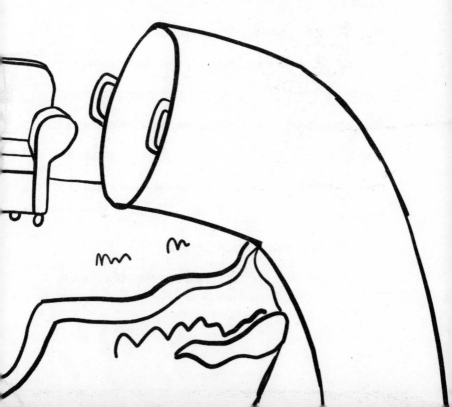

HOW TO SAIL A PRETEND PIRATE SHIP

The sofa went under, and we went with it. I'd been screaming all the way down and my breath was almost gone. Myrt twisted out of my arms in panic and I kicked upwards, desperate for air.

I quickly broke the surface, but Johnnie was on top of me before I could even catch a proper breath. And then Myrt was scrambling on as well, and it was all I could do to keep my head above water. But even through all the panic, I managed to shout at Johnnie.

'You idiot, we're gonna drown!'

The shore was only five metres away, but the tide

was sucking us away from the beach and Johnnie can't even begin to swim. Most pretend pirates on pretend pirate ships would have drowned at this point. But Johnnie's ship, I discovered between shouting, was . . . real. The brown sofa had been adapted, and it came crashing back up to the surface with a loud, bubbling roar.

And the next minute we were back aboard; my brain was still shouting, but my mouth stopped when a telescopic pole emerged from deep within the springs. There was the sound of air tanks releasing gas while Johnnie fiddled with a TV remote control. A sail billowed out and Johnnie looked pleased. And then, with a whine of electric engines, the boat lurched forward.

Johnnie turned to look at my shocked face.

'What did you think Dad and I were doing all this time?'

Myrt looked fierce – she hates being wet – but made herself comfortable and started chewing on her back leg.[6] Johnnie used his remote to set a course for the mid-Atlantic.

'Easy,' he said with the confidence of a five-year-old.

'Easy,' I quietly repeated with the zero confidence of a ten-year-old.

You might think that surviving a nine-metre sofa crash would give me confidence, all the confidence in the world, even. You might think that discovering we had a real boat with a solar sail and electric engines and a top speed of eighteen knots (which meant we could get to the island in just over eleven hours!) would be a good thing.

---

6   Don't ask me why; I think she does it to relax.

But it wasn't.

All those months and years of playing pirates with Dad and Johnnie, and neither of them had ever mentioned that they were making a real ship. As if I was too stupid to help. Too stupid to even be told the truth. We sailed all morning, and all morning it was all I could think about.

'It's my turn, OK?' I eventually said. 'Give me the remote.' My voice sounded robotic. Not like me at all.

Johnnie clenched his jaw. 'No-K, Eliza. I'm the captain.'

'It's – my – turn,' I repeated. 'Give – me – the – remote.' My voice was deeper.

'NO, it's mine.'

I grabbed his chubby little arm and squeezed. He cried out, but he just wouldn't let go of the control. So I squeezed harder.

He screamed and ripped his arm away, and the remote flipped over the back of the sofa into the sea. I jumped up in time to see it jerking and lurching downwards. Down deep until it was lost in the green ocean.

The boat stopped instantly.

Johnnie's face was pink with rage. 'You've ruined *everything*!' he shouted.

And then the narwhal attacked. And ruined everything.

HOW TO SURVIVE A NARWHAL ATTACK

Unicorn of the sea? That's just advertising.

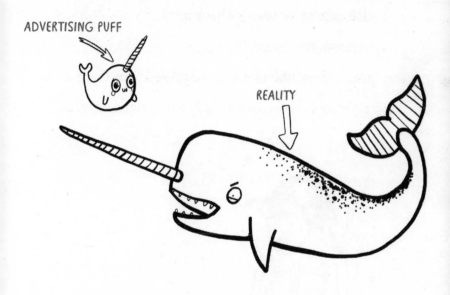

ADVERTISING PUFF

REALITY

Even before it'd got a brown sofa stuck on its horn, this one was angry. The narwhal thrashed about, smacking the side of our boat into the water, and then took the sofa down. Down deep in a death roll. We were lucky to be flung off, but it still had a good go at killing the brown sofa.

I resurfaced to see Johnnie struggling to keep his face above the water. And he was turning anticlockwise because of his leg.

'Scared but doing it, scared but doing it,' he repeated over and over in a breathless little voice.

I grabbed one of his hands and he looked grateful. Myrt doggy-paddled to us with a crazed look in her

eye. She climbed on to my head, scratching with her claws and drawing blood as she scrambled up my face. My brain was racing.

Johnnie gripped on to me hard. He was blowing hard too to avoid swallowing water, but he smiled between blows. He squeezed my hands three times – it was our special code for 'I love you'.

'Dolphins,' he said, as if that made sense. 'Do the volume.' He pointed at Myrt with wild eyes. 'The collar!'

You can imagine my confusion.

Then the narwhal was back. Horn first, then sofa, and then a huge white rubbery-blubbery body covered in bright red blobs.

It breached the surface and would have come crashing down on us, but the narwhal twisted and turned, smashing down into the sea with a whump that shook the ocean.

And then it was gone again.

Johnnie wriggled his hand free of mine and grabbed at Myrt. She yelped as he dragged her into the water. I saw him reaching for her collar. And then, with a look of horror on both our faces, he started sinking.

'Johnnie!'

I screamed as I dived after him, but he was going down like a rock. I emptied my lungs to make myself less buoyant and kicked down with all my strength. But there were strange black shapes in the gloom below. My chest cramped and I shouted in horror, bubbles everywhere. I kicked upwards in terror and broke the surface with a cry.

And immediately realized, with a sudden flattening dread, that I'd let my baby brother drown.

HOW TO MAKE IT UP TO SOMEONE FOR LETTING THEM DOWN/DROWN

Myrt was nowhere to be seen either. I looked left and right for any sign of anyone or anything, but I was alone, utterly alone. There was no one left, just me. And as if I had lead in my heart, I sank.

Going down this time was strangely peaceful. As I sank deeper, and the light began to fade, creatures big and small flashed by.

I felt the tightness in my chest return. Then I saw a dolphin as it dipped between my legs. A bottlenose, like the ones you see on the telly.

And then another, and another. Before long there were dozens of them, shooting round me in a flurry of bubbles.

The world turned and so did I. Faster and faster. Blinded by bubbles, I knew with sudden horror what was happening. The dolphins had trapped me in a bubble net. Even they were against me.

But when the whole world is spinning there's no time for terror. There's not even time to realize you're going upwards, back towards the surface.

All you can do is propel your vom as far as you can so it doesn't come slapping back into your face. And with one giant heave I was shot out of the water vortex and into the air.

And slap back down on to our big brown sofa next to a soggy-looking Johnnie and an angry-looking Myrt. The dolphins had rescued them too.

There was a narwhal-horn-sized hole in the middle and the cushions were soaked through, but otherwise it looked remarkably familiar. The dolphins now seemed as happy as anything, bobbing up and down in the water, making clickety, whistley noises and looking like they wanted us to feed them sushi.

Then I saw the narwhal. It loomed over us, massive but strangely calm. And now it was close by I could better see the dozens of red splodges all over its face and body.

That bizarre sight posed several questions.

I poked one of the red splodges with my finger

and it twisted to reveal two huge innocent eyes.

'Awww,' I said, 'it's so cute.'

And then this happened:

'Vampire squid!' shouted Johnnie unhelpfully late. Myrt went mad and I watched in horrified fascination as the red splodge dropped off the face of the narwhal and buried itself into a sofa cushion. Its little body pulsed and sucked, as it searched for more blood.

HOW TO SAVE A NARWHAL FROM VAMPIRE SQUID

You're probably wondering what to do in a situation like this. Vampire squid aren't normally like this – they live on plankton and stuff that's already dead. But there was something different about this one.

'It's got a BIN!' said Johnnie, clearly excited.

I didn't understand immediately, but Johnnie poked at a tiny coil of wire coming out of its head. 'A Brain Interface Node? Like Dad invented? But aren't they banned?'

'Maybe nobody told the vampire squid,' said Johnnie.

'So you're saying this squid is a . . .' I trailed off, and Johnnie finished my sentence.

'It's a biobot, Eliza. Part animal, part computer. That thing is artificially intelligent.'

'Really?' I gave it another poke, but it just carried on sucking at the cushion.

We looked back at the narwhal, and sure enough there were coils on the other blobs too, maybe all of them.

Johnnie's eyes were glinting with excitement.

'A single biobot may be a bit dim, but use the BIN to link them up in a network, and they could get super intelligent. Maybe the brainiest thing on the planet.'

'You're telling me this thing is the brainiest thing on the planet?' The squid was still sucking on the cushion.

Johnnie shrugged. 'Maybe there's no Wi-Fi here.'

I looked at the narwhal. Its giant eye was horribly sad. And the red blobs on its body were still pulsing away. We had to do something.

'We've got to get these things off,' I said. But, as usual, Johnnie was already way ahead of me.

Now, you probably have no idea how to rescue a narwhal from artificially intelligent vampire squid. But don't worry, Johnnie has submitted a chapter to the publishers of *The Book of Secrets* in the hope it will make it into the next edition. So when it gets published you can learn from our trial and error.

If you've ever heard narwhal song, you'll know how easy it is to understand. Every squid we flicked into that lunchbox was met with a little peal of joy. There were eleven altogether, and Johnnie insisted on keeping them all, 'As evidence'.[7]

'But evidence of what?' That was the big

_____

7   I also think he liked the idea of having weird new pets.

question. Why on Earth had these biobot squid things ended up sucking on a narwhal in the middle of the Atlantic Ocean?

By the time we'd finished, even though it was getting dark, we could see the look of gratitude in the narwhal's solemn blue eyes. We'd made a friend.

'Dad would love this,' I said to Johnnie. 'He always wanted us to go swimming with a narwhal. But I always said no. I thought they'd squash us.'

I watched the narwhal as it swam in a gentle figure of eight next to our little boat. We'd done a science project on narwhals at school. They used to live in the Arctic, but ever since everything up there melted back in the 2030s, they've been spotted everywhere, all over the planet. Like they'd evolved overnight to live in warmer oceans.

Warmer oceans, that was just something else to worry about.

'If we get Mum and Dad back, I promise I'll never worry again,' I whispered, making my promise to the universe. But even I didn't believe it.

I tried to call them, of course. My phone was waterproof, but every time I checked it there was no signal.

We tried to get the engines working again, but with the sun setting and the light going it was impossible. So that night we drifted, lost in the middle of the black ocean. There was nothing to be done but wait for morning.

When you're that far from land, you get to see every single one of the 250 billion stars in the Milky Way pop back into existence.

'There's Mars,' said Johnnie, pointing.

'Mars is a planet, not a star,' I said, but Johnnie just shrugged as if I was stupid.

'How do you know anyway?' I eventually asked.

because that's Sagittarius,' he said, as if that explained everything.

'Knowing about stars doesn't make you better than me, you know.'

I turned my back on him, but soon felt him shuffle up close. In the dark I could feel him rubbing his leg. Mum usually does that for him, and I could tell from his huffing and puffing that his short little arms were struggling.

'How's your leg?' I asked, knowing what would come next.

'It's really achy . . . . Can you do Mum's rubbing thing?'

So we sat beneath the open sky and I rubbed

Johnnie's leg while he taught me about the stars and how Sagittarius actually looks like a teapot with its spout pointing at Mars. And, now I thought about it, Mars didn't look like a twinkly star at all. It looked red and round, like a burning fireball. Why would anyone want to leave Earth to go there?

'You're even better than Mum at this,' Johnnie said after about ten minutes of rubbing. It was one

of the nicest things Johnnie's ever said to me, so I kept going.

'And you're miles better than Dad. Dad fell asleep once.' After a pause Johnnie asked, 'Do you think we'll ever see them again?'

'Of course we will,' I lied.

'I knew you'd say that. Dad always called you the Girl Who Never Gives Up.'

I felt tears prick my eyes and it took a while to trust my voice. He used to call me that, but he hadn't said it for a long time.

'Let's get some sleep,' I said eventually. We settled down, with Myrt in the middle to keep us warm. And I fell asleep calculating the fifty trillion ways we could fail.

HOW TO OVERCOME ODDS OF FIFTY TRILLION TO ONE

The next morning, Johnnie made sun-dried seaweed for breakfast. Myrt wouldn't touch it.

While we ate, I told Johnnie how bad the odds were of ever seeing our parents again. I thought he'd cry, but he just chewed his seaweed in silence.

We'd drifted a long way in the night, but the dolphins were back and the narwhal had hung around too. Somehow, with them around, things didn't seem quite so bad.

'Have you tried your phone this morning?' Johnnie asked.

'Of course I have,' I lied. 'But I'll try again.'

I called Mum first. Nothing. So I tried Dad, but without much hope. And then, like some miracle, his face appeared. It was pixelated and distorted but definitely Dad.

'Hi, kiddos! How're you doing?'

I screamed. Johnnie came rushing over.

'Dad! We're coming to rescue you! Where are you?'

Johnnie was jumping up and down on his weak little legs and I felt tears running down my face.

There was no answer. The screen had frozen.

'Dad!' I shouted. And then suddenly he was back, the picture much clearer. It was all so weird. He was outside in the brilliant sunshine with rainforest all around.

'Dad, where are you? We're coming to rescue you!'

'What do you mean, you're coming to rescue us?'

He looked genuinely confused and for a moment I was lost for words.

'But, Daddy,' said Johnnie, 'we got your message.'

On the screen Dad frowned, looking confused. 'What message? Guys, we're going to *Mars*. Mr Noah's given us the Chance of a Lifetime.' He turned his phone to show us a launch pad, with three identical rockets lined up in a neat row.

'I wish you'd stop saying that, Dad.'

I didn't know what to say next. I looked at Johnnie. His chin was wobbling. We both stood there staring at the phone. Dad smiled back at us like some kind of robot.

And then he did the strangest thing. He put the phone down on the ground, so all we could see was blue sky. It seemed likes ages, but suddenly he was back, smiling like before but with a marker pen behind his ear. And then the screen shifted again, showing the base of the pyramid. We could make out two words in black ink. The writing was so rubbish, we could barely read it.

COME QUICK

'*Come quick,*' Johnnie read out loud.

Then Dad's face was back. And suddenly Mum was there too.

'Mummy!' I hadn't called her that since I was five years old, but it just came out.

She smiled and I touched the screen with my hand, touching her face. 'Mum, you have to stop the launch.'

'Don't be silly, honey, this is the Chance of a Lifetime.'

I wanted to scream.

'Be nice to each other,' she finished. 'We have to go now. Byeee.'

And that was it. The picture just froze.

I was shaking.

Johnnie had his face buried in Myrt's neck, but I could tell he was crying.

He was crying but there was nothing I could do; I just couldn't take my eyes off that frozen picture of Mum and Dad. It was the last time I'd ever see them, smiling and happy, like we were all going on holiday together.

And then I saw it.

I blinked hard to clear my tears, not daring to believe what I was seeing.

'Johnnie, look at this.'

Johnnie's red blotchy face shot up immediately.

'Look.'

I showed him the screen and Johnnie reached out to touch Mum's face with his chubby little finger.

'Look at her neck.'

Johnnie stared, but he wasn't seeing it.

'Look, it's just like the vampire squid,' I said.

Johnnie zoomed in, then zoomed in more, until he saw it. At the base of Mum's head was a miniscule coil of wire.

I looked at Johnnie and he looked at me and we both nodded.

'She's got a BIN,' I said breathlessly. 'Their brains are plugged into a computer.'

'Mum and Dad didn't get rid of us,' said Johnnie, smiling. 'They've been hacked.'

Suddenly Johnnie's expression changed. 'I need the poop deck,' he said, and trundled off to the back of the boat.

I turned my back. Nobody wants to see that.

With Johnnie on the poop deck, I had time to think.

I knew all about computer hacking. There's a whole chapter on it in *The Book of Secrets*.[8] And, besides, Sadie Snickpick had once hacked my Singalonga Disney Princess doll. She'd changed the

---

8 See **Secret 37: How to Hack Stuff and Take Over the World**, *The Book of Secrets*.

song to 'Eliza is a Buttface'. It just sang and sang until the batteries ran out.

Things were beginning to make sense. If Mum and Dad had been hacked through the computer BIN thingy in their brains, then it would explain everything: why they looked more spaced out than usual; why they'd been less huggy; why they were leaving us to go to their certain death on an alien planet. *Everything.* It was just so typical of my dad to invent something and then get hacked through his own invention.

I thought about my hacked Disney doll. We'd had to get rid of it in the end. But who would hack a real-life human being? And why would they bother with my mum and dad?

And most importantly of all: can you unhack a hacked human?

I stewed on that for ages (Johnnie may be a

genius, but he takes for ever to pull his pants up).
Would we rescue Mum and Dad only to find out
they were mindless zombies for ever?'

My mind spun into a spiral of despair. The biobot
vampire squid were making horrible, squelchy
noises in Johnnie's lunchbox and I looked at the
gashes they'd left on the narwhal. Had they been

trying to burrow into the narwhal's brain too? Who would want to hack a narwhal? And why?

'I know what wrote on the back of the letter, and on the pyramid,' said Johnnie, interrupting my circling thoughts. He was back from the poop deck and he was smiling.

I made him wash his hands in the sea.

'You mean, *who*?' I said impatiently.

'No, *what*.'

'What?'

'Exactly. It was Dad's right brain.'

'His *right* brain?'

'Yeah, I think they've hacked all of Mum's brain, but only half of Dad's. I think they've only managed to hack the left side.'

Now, none of this made sense, so I got Johnnie to draw me a diagram in my journal. It explained everything.

I looked at Johnnie. 'I still don't get it.'

He took a breath and said, 'There's a famous experiment, in which someone had their brain cut in half and they asked them to write down what job they wanted. One hand wrote "accountant", but the other hand wrote . . . "racing driver".'

'They cut someone's brain in half?'

'Well, yeah, sometimes doctors do that . . . to make you better.'

'Doctors sometimes cut your brain in half to make you better?' I was appalled. As if I didn't have enough to worry about.

'Just forget that bit. It doesn't matter *why* their

brain was cut in half, the point is we all have two halves to our brain, and it looks like Dad's only been half hacked.'

I pulled a face while I thought about it, but Johnnie was impatient to get on.

'Come on, we need to get to the island.'

'Johnnie, it's still a million miles away. And the engines have stopped if you hadn't noticed.'

But Johnnie had a map up on my phone. 'Look,' he said, pointing at the coordinates, 'we must have drifted in the night. It's only about forty miles away.'

Myrt barked. And, as if they'd been listening all along, the dolphins leapt out of the sea, spraying us with salt water.

Johnnie was instantly full of can-do, and for once it didn't annoy me. Together we came up with a new plan:

NEW PLAN

Mend our broken boat
= ~~1 in 1,000~~
Ask dolphins for a tow =
easy-peasy lemon-squeezy

Get to island before Mum
and Dad's rocket takes off
~~= 1 in 100,000~~
It's only 40 miles! =
Easy-peasy ham + cheesy

Stop vampire squid eating their way
out of a lunchbox and eating our
faces = ~~1 in 100~~
Let them eat each other! = Easy-peasy
pick your nose and make it sneezy

Make Mum and Dad want
us again = ~~1 in 1,000~~
= Easy-peasy eat loads of butter
and your sick gets greasy

Get home safe = ~~1 in 5~~
Easy-peasy when you fart your
pants get breezy

Overall probability = ~~1 in~~
~~50,000,000,000,000~~
Somewhere between doable
and a doddle

So there it was, not fifty trillion to one at all. But somewhere between doable and a doddle.

You might be thinking Johnnie was being a touch optimistic.

You might be thinking we'd stumble at 'ask dolphins for a tow'.

But you're wrong.

Wrongy wrong, wrong, wrong.

You see, what I didn't understand until Johnnie explained it very carefully, is that Myrt could speak Dolphin.

HOW TO TALK DOLPHIN

The conversation went something like this:

It was typical Dad, inventing things that no one needed. I mean, when does a dog *ever* need to talk to a dolphin? A human perhaps, and definitely a cat. But a dolphin?

Except without that collar, we'd already be at the bottom of the Atlantic. So maybe parents aren't as stupid as they look.

I listened to the squeaks and clacks and whistles coming out of Myrt's collar, convinced it wouldn't work. But not for long, because moments later we were all set. You can see why they think dolphins

are going to take over the planet when we go extinct.

That morning, despite everything, I felt hope. We shot along (Johnnie reckoned we got up to eight knots). The dolphins and the narwhal made a huge trough in the ocean as they ploughed us towards the island. And the wind in my face seemed to blow the worst of my worries away. For a moment at least.

Don't get me wrong, things were bad, really bad, but we were at least going in the right direction. Mum and Dad were getting closer, eight miles[9] closer every hour. And we knew what the problem was, even if we didn't know how to solve it.

Johnnie spent most of the morning studying Dad's map and eventually I sat down next to him and asked the question that had been bugging me for a day and a bit.

'So, this Noah, who is he again?'

---

9 Correction! 8 nautical miles an hour. J

Johnnie sighed melodramatically, but I ignored it.

'And why does he only have one name?'

'How can you not know who Noah is? Do you even watch the news?'

Sometimes you have to just put up with this sort of thing from Johnnie, if you want to get to the good stuff. Johnnie spoke and I made notes in my journal. If we were going to rescue Mum and Dad from a top-secret island, then I wanted to know something about the man who owned it.

At the time I didn't know what to make of the mysterious Mr Noah. Was he an evil criminal who'd hacked our mum and dad? Or a good guy who'd given Mum and Dad the chance to go into space? In case you follow the news as much as I used to (i.e. not) it probably makes sense to give you a bit of background.

A BIT OF BACKGROUND ON THE MYSTERIOUS MR NOAH

Potholes.

It all started with potholes. Yep, potholes. In the road. One winter there were millions of extra potholes on every road in every country on the planet – something to do with climate change, probably. The traffic jams got worse, and worse, until . . . .

This is a pothole

↓

The big jam.

All around the world, traffic ground to a halt. People were stuck in their cars for weeks, months. It was bad everywhere, until . . .

The flying taxi.

Noah launched his flying car. But you couldn't buy them; you could only hire them. They had robot drivers and they could go anywhere.

Noah became the world's richest man in less than a year.

'I also read somewhere that he earns $1,000,000 a second, and gives half of it to charity,' Johnnie added.

'He doesn't sound evil.'

'Evil is as evil does,' said Johnnie with a solemn look.

'What does that mean?' I asked. But I never found out.

Because then, just after noon, Myrt spotted the island.

She howled into the blue sky and I grabbed Johnnie's telescope to see a jungle-covered paradise with a pyramid piercing the trees at its heart.

'Cross it off the list, Johnster! We've found the island!'

I felt tingles in my arms and hands. For a bit, just a little bit, I felt invincible.

The sun was high and it lit up the white-sand

beach with sparkles. As perfect a beach as you could hope to see, with mangos, coconut palms and bright pink flowers everywhere. I passed the telescope to Johnnie and he swore he could even see an ice-cream kiosk. It was all so gorgeous, as lovely a scene as you could ever dream in a million dreams.

And maybe because of that, or maybe because a cloud went across the sun, I felt a sudden shiver of dread.

The big, obvious problem was that to get to this idyllic beach you had to go between two giant outcrops of rock.

'The Clashing Rocks,' said Johnnie, reading from Dad's map. 'Do you think they're real?'

We'd been brought up on Dad's stories of Greek heroes whose boats had been smashed to pieces by magical rocks that somehow crashed together.

I double-checked the map. It was pretty clear that this was the only way in.

HOW TO CONQUER CLASHING ROCKS

There's an obvious way to test if Clashing Rocks are actually real. Send in a bird and see what happens.

We couldn't find a bird, but tried something kind of similar. The rocks were definitely real.

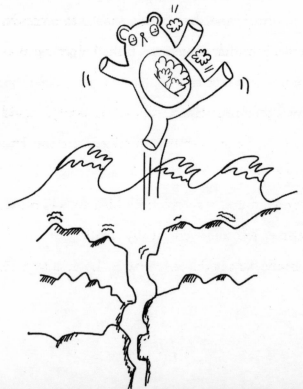

The rocks snapped back into position within seconds, primed and ready. Clashing rock tech has obviously come on a bit since ancient Greece.

'I think they're real,' said Johnnie quietly.

We'd found the island – exactly where Dad's map said it was – only to find it was impossible to get on to.

I had another look at the map. There had to be something, some clue left by Dad. He gave it to Johnnie for a reason. He must have known something might happen to him, before he was hacked.

'We could try the Cliffs of Insanity?' said Johnnie, looking over my shoulder. 'Or the Fire Swamp?'

I turned round and took both his hands in mine. Sometimes Johnnie seems really small.

'Johnnie, this is the only way in. Look, it says so

right there in Dad's writing.'

Johnnie's eyes were welling up. 'But Mum and Dad?'

'We'll think of something,' I said, but I knew we'd failed. We had time – the rocket launch was still a whole day away – but we were totally stuck, bobbing about half a mile from the shore.

The Clashing Rocks meant certain death.

It was truly, horribly stupid to even think about trying to get through them.

And then Myrt did something even more truly, horribly stupid than that.

A clownfish just happened to swim by. Myrt gave one angry growl, and went straight in after it.

You remember me telling you that Myrt sometimes bites people? Especially when they're wearing orange? Well, it's time I explained why.

You see, Myrt is a dog who likes to hold a grudge.

WHY MYRT IS THE ANGRIEST SPANIEL

Myrt was a happy-go-lucky puppy.
The cutest thing you've ever seen.
When she came to US, she was no
bigger than my dad's shoe.

But then, one
fine spring day,
everything changed.
We were watching
Finding Nemo on
TV when this
happened:

Lucky for me she
never realized it was
my fault. Instead
Myrt blamed the
clownfish.

And she's been
angry ever since;
Clownfish are her
nemesis (Nemosis??)

She just has to
see orange and
it sets her off.
My dad learned
the hard way
to avoid orange
underpants.

So, when Myrt saw her 'Nemosis' in the water, a real-life actual clownfish, she was off and in. Straight in, and straight at it. And it was going straight for the Clashing Rocks.

Johnnie was useless. He just stood there mouthing 'Myrt' over and over. And then finally he turned to me with such horrible desperation and pleaded softly, 'Do something, 'Liza.'

Myrt kept disappearing beneath the waves, only for her little head to pop back up moments later. Then she reached the rocks. They smashed together with a hideous *crack* of stone on stone. And Myrt disappeared completely.

Johnnie let out a wail.

He'd known her all his life.

His Myrty. Was gone.

And then, as the rocks drew back, her head bobbed up again on the other side.

'She made it!' screamed Johnnie, and he turned and hugged me tight with his short little arms until we were both crying and hugging each other.

'She went *underneath*,' I mumbled through my tears and Johnnie nodded. At that moment my imagination told me everything I needed to know: *The Clashing Rocks don't work under water.*

Now you probably think turning a sofa pirate ship into a submarine is easy. Just let some air out of the tanks and sink it a bit. But it doesn't work like that. Johnnie tried, of course, but quickly decided it was impossible. And, besides, with Myrt gone, our only way of communicating with the dolphins had gone too. There was no way of coordinating anything.

But there was one answer. And I knew exactly what we had to do.

'We have to trust the dolphins,' I said.

Johnnie looked dubious, and for once it was nice to be a step ahead of him.

'Dolphins rescue people. It's their nature. It's what they do. We just have to jump, abandon ship, and let them take us to shore.'

We cut free the dolphins and the narwhal, and secured our rucksacks as best we could.

Johnnie jumped first, with just the smallest of pushes. As he flapped about in the water, I watched and waited for the rescue.

It's instinct, you see; dolphins can't help it even if they want to. They see somebody who needs rescuing, and they're on it.

Johnnie had to wait less than twenty seconds before one of the dolphins brought him back to the surface. He clung on, riding it like a wet jockey on a slippery horse. And with a rescue instinct second to none, it was gone, heading for the safety of the beach at 20 miles per hour. Only 300 tonnes of smashing rocks stood in their way.

At this point you may be thinking that we were putting rather a lot of trust in a mere marine mammal. But that just shows how stupid humans are. Dolphins are *not* mere marine mammals.

Let me explain:

So when the rocks clashed, the dolphins' echolocation spotted it in less than a second. They knew the shape of the rock, where to go for safety, how fast to move, all in the time it takes you to pick your nose and check if anyone's watching.

Johnnie reappeared seconds later. And less than

a minute after jumping off the boat, he'd joined a bedraggled-looking Myrt on the beach. She was eating an ice cream, and moments later so was he.

Now it was my turn. I looked into the clear blue water. It was so clear I could see the bottom. But for the life of me I couldn't jump. My brain said: 'Trust in the dolphins, you'll be fine.' But the rest of me disagreed.

And if the narwhal hadn't given me a nudge, I think I'd still be on that sofa. Sometimes in life you just need a little shove.

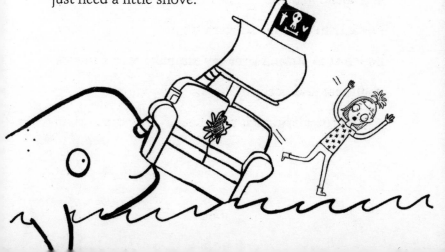

'That's the best ice cream I've ever tasted,' was all I could say after I joined Johnnie on the beach.

'There's more, you know,' explained Johnnie. 'The robot chimp makes it fresh.'

I stared at the chimp. After the two days we'd just had, nothing surprised me any more.

'How do you know it's a robot?'

'Look at the way it walks.'

Once he'd said that, it was obvious. The chimp walked on two legs but like a puppet without strings.

'Johnnie, we don't have time for this. I know the launch is tomorrow but we still have to cross the rainforest and—'

'Shush!' Johnnie shouted.

He was staring over my shoulder and I turned, but there was nothing.

And then I heard it too.

Beyond the ice-cream kiosk, beyond the hedge of flowers and the rainforest beyond, I heard a noise.

'This is bad,' he said.

The noise grew louder and it was unmistakable. It was the noise of a rocket engine firing into life.

'This is bad,' I said, which was the understatement of the century. Mum and Dad's rocket was launching early.

Was this the end of the world?

HOW TO SURVIVE THE END OF THE WORLD

We heard the engines firing in blasts, getting louder each time. I'd seen a rocket launch before on TV, and I recognized the rhythmic pattern with heart-stopping certainty. I could even hear the countdown in my head.

Ten, nine, eight . . .

I looked at Johnnie, his cheeks and mouth covered in chocolate, his eyes filled with tears. The engines fired again and again, and the voice in my head counted on. I could imagine it playing out on screens all over the world.

Four, three, two, one . . . Engage booster ignition . . .

Then nothing.

Total silence.

Myrt ran, off the beach and into the jungle.

For one intense moment I thought it was all a false alarm. But then booster rockets engaged, and I knew my life was over.

The noise came rumbling across the island like a typhoon, building louder and louder. Trees bent like grass, and coconuts fell like rain. Johnnie stuck his squidgy little hands over his ears and the noise grew so thick my own ears stabbed with pain.

Weirdly close a rocket seemed to wobble up into the air. With obvious effort it lifted from the ground. Out of the rainforest and into the clear blue Atlantic sky. Impossibly loud, impossibly big, hanging in mid-air.

And then it was gone. And smoke was everywhere.

Johnnie was speaking but I couldn't hear what

he was saying. My ears were ringing so loud that I couldn't even hear him crying. I grabbed him, like Mum would have done, and squeezed him tight. He was all I had left. My family, my life, this crazy adventure, everything, it was all over.

HOW TO GET OVER IT BEING ALL OVER

We stayed like that for a long time. Maybe we were too afraid to let go of each other. Maybe we just didn't know what to say or do next. When we did stop hugging, Johnnie was strangely calm. Myrt was back, and we just sat there letting her lick us.

We checked my phone, of course. The newsfeed summed it up in one quick sentence: **NOAH: MARS MISSION GOES DAY EARLY**.

I chucked the stupid thing into the sea and regretted it immediately. But the chimp was already bringing more ice creams, so we just sat and ate them.

'We could stay here for a bit, you know,' I said, looking up at the mango trees and the lychees and the soft pink flowers on the vines all around.

Johnnie looked up. He had an ice-cream smile but not a real one.

'Everybody loves mango,' he said, looking at a tree full of them without any joy. 'And there's a banana plantation on the map, remember? Bananas are a complete food – you can live on just bananas for ever.'

Without being asked the robot chimp brought us more ice cream. This one was banana and mango, and the chimp squeezed goo from a small green fruit all over it. It oozed down the ice cream like honey, but sweeter.

'Let's just stay here. Like, for ever,' said Johnnie.

And he had a point. Mum and Dad were gone. There was no reason to keep going. And what was there to go back home for?

And so the afternoon trundled on, in a blur of ice cream and snoozing on sunloungers and exploring the beach, and in the warm shallows Johnnie found some turtle eggs and we watched them for a bit. We'd had enough adventure. People always tell you not to give up. Dad might have called me the Girl Who Never Gives Up, but giving up now was strangely peaceful.

Eventually the sun set on Day 2. The robot chimp produced some sleeping bags from somewhere and lit a campfire. It was idyllic in a way. The sand was warm and the air cool, Myrt slept and the insects sang. And then Johnnie dropped his bombshell.

'I love it when you're not cross with me, Eliza.'

I was immediately cross with him. 'That's stupid. I'm never cross with you.'

Johnnie went quiet, and that made me even madder.

'Why do you always have to ruin things? Everything was fine, and then you have to start an argument. You're so annoying.'

'Is that why you don't like me?' he said in a small voice.

'What do you mean? Of course I like you. You're my brother. Why wouldn't I like you? I have to like you.' I was rambling, and we both knew it.

'It's just . . . you always get so cross,' he said.

'No, I don't, you dum-dum.'

Johnnie didn't say anything. Which always unnerves me.

'Well, I'm not angry now, am I?' I said with finality.

But his eyes looked big and black by the light of the campfire. Even in the dark I could see tears.

I took a moment and then decided to tell him the truth.

'It's not easy having a genius baby brother, you know.'

He didn't say anything, just stared. And suddenly it all came tumbling out of me.

'Mum and Dad used to play with me all the time; they thought I was the best thing in the universe until you came along. Now I'm second best. Everything I do, or want to do, you've done already or you're better at, or you're going to be better at any minute. I'm just a monster who doesn't share, who needs to grow up and "be more like Johnnie". You're the genius, but I'm the one who always has to be more grown-up. Think about it. It's hard . . .'

'Hard to like me?' Johnnie's voice was small.

'Yes . . . no . . . I don't mean . . . I mean . . .'

'I see,' was all he said after that, but I could see proper tears now.

I was a monster.

My brain did gymnastics trying to think how to make things right. I watched little Johnnie disappearing inside his sleeping bag. He wobbled about like a caterpillar in a chrysalis.

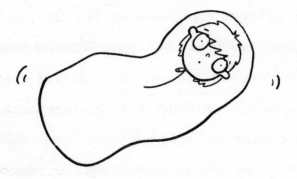

Eventually I put my arm out and gave him a cuddle.

'Sorry, Johnnie. I shouldn't have said that. There's so much to like.' But by then he was fast asleep.

Myrt gave me a look, and then curled up next to him.

HOW TO ESCAPE FROM AN ICE-CREAM PARADISE TRAP

On the morning of Day 3 I woke from a terrible dream, gasping for air. Mum and Dad were sinking to the bottom of the ocean, reaching out for me to save them. But when I grabbed them, they dragged me under.

The robot chimp brought ice cream (coconut, mango, lychee and more of that green honey fruit) and I immediately felt calmer. Johnnie seemed to have forgotten our conversation from the day before; he was busy looking at Dad's map. Myrt was eating a double scoop of mango and strawberry, and for the first time in as long as I can remember, she didn't look angry.

'We could stay here another day,' I said, 'just to build our strength up.'

Johnnie nodded in agreement as the chimp brought a second helping. The sun was already hot and we moved into the shade of a palm tree, feeling the warm sand between our bare toes. My brain felt numb. I actually felt happy. All my worries seemed a thousand miles away.

And that's when I knew something was terribly wrong.

This wasn't paradise.

This was a trap.

My imagination ran wild: me, Johnnie and Myrt, so stuffed full of ice cream that we couldn't even move. Super-advanced robot apes were rolling us across the sand and into cages.

'Johnnie, I think we're in a trap.'

He screwed up his face and gave a little grunt through a mouthful of ice cream. Myrt was wriggling contentedly in the sand and licking mango ice cream off her paws. *Orange* mango ice cream.

I was right, something was very wrong.

'Johnnie, we need to go. Now.'

'What's the point? Mum and Dad must be half a million miles away by now. What are we gonna do, build a rocket and chase after them?'

'I don't know, maybe we can turn their rocket round or steal one. There were three, remember?'

'Don't be stupid. That's so totally impossible.'

I looked at Johnnie as he went back to his ice cream.

'Whatever, baby brother, but we need to get off this beach. Watch.'

I stood. RoboChimp immediately whirred into action and stood too. I took a step towards the edge of the beach and the robot looked on, obviously alert. Another step, and then another, and the chimp was on his shop till. Before I could step off the beach, he was beside me, gesticulating wildly at a receipt. He handed it to me and I read it with horror.

The chimp looked fierce, so I just smiled and went back to Johnnie. I showed him the receipt.

'See. It's a trap. We need to get out of here.'

RoboChimp brought another mango ice cream, and I took it without hesitation. The chimp seemed satisfied and went back to its kiosk.

I mouthed to Johnnie, 'How do we escape from a robot chimp with an unpaid ice-cream bill?'

Johnnie nodded; he knew exactly what to do. He went straight to *The Book of Secrets*. **Secret 106: How to Outsmart a Robot**. It might seem stupid but for the first time in my life I realized something quite important. Johnnie was on my side. He wasn't the enemy. And it was stupid to keep turning him into one.

I read the page quickly.

I was smiling by the time I got to the bottom of the page. If there's one thing I'm better at than anyone, it's imagination. Imagination is my thing. For once in my life I felt the hot glow of supreme confidence.

SECRET 106: HOW TO OUTSMART A ROBOT

Everybody Knows: Even old people know robots rely on computer algorithms, step-by-step instructions that tell the computer exactly what to do. That was bad for robot makers because they had to think of every possible situation in advance and create instructions to cope with all those situations. So someone invented 'Machine Learning' where the robot learns things all by itself and improves by trial and error.

But Secret 106 is this: Machine Learning has its limits; even the cleverest robot hasn't been in every possible situation. Humans still have an edge when it comes to imagination. If you want to outsmart a robot, just imagine a situation it hasn't been in. It's sure to do something really stupid.

Practical Know-how:
If you need to beat a chess computer: use backgammon pieces.

If you need to outsmart a robot lawnmower that's trying to cut your toes off: step off the grass.

If you need to escape from an ice-cream-selling robot without paying: ask it for an impossible combination of flavours and sneak out while it's looking for them.

I looked over to the chimp at the kiosk, and without a second's hesitation said loudly, 'Could I have seahorse-glitter and mermaid-poo flavour, please?'

And with even less hesitation the robot chimp was gone. Last seen walking down the beach and into the sea. I assume it was waterproof.

'That was amazing,' said Johnnie, and for once I believed it. 'You totally whupped that robot. Dad always said you were the fiercest pirate ever.'

I looked at Johnnie. 'You're joking me?'

'No. He said you weren't afraid of anything when you were small. He said you saved him from a lion's mane jellyfish once, a real one.'

I shook my head. 'Did Dad really say that? About me?'

Johnnie nodded, then his voice went squeaky with laughter. 'You were only zero, you weren't even one, and you chucked some Lego at it, and it started choking and stopped stinging Dad.'

I didn't remember any of that. But then why would I? I was only zero.

But then I had a sudden flash of memory of being on a real boat with a red sail and a blue sky. We were on a sailing adventure. Dad was wearing his pirate outfit and he had big, red sting-marks across his face. He was smiling like it was the best day in the history of the world.

The memory evaporated with a single thought. 'So why did he stop having adventures with me?'

'I dunno. You said you were too old.'

'I didn't say that.'

'Yes, you did. I heard you.'

I didn't know what to say. I hadn't said that, had I?

Maybe I had.

But Johnnie was already off, back to check on his turtle eggs from yesterday.

'Do you think we can take one of these eggs with us?' asked Johnnie.

'Best not,' I said. 'It's probably really bad to move them.'

And before RoboChimp could bring us back a mermaid poo, we slipped through a thick hedge of pink flowers, and into the jungly interior.

HOW TO SURVIVE IN A RAINFOREST

After the cool, calm, breezy, sunny beach, the rainforest was hot, humid, dark and noisy. The thing they don't tell you in books is that jungles are covered in cobwebs. And I mean *covered*. Rainforests are full of bugs, and where there are bugs there are spiders to eat them. And where there are spiders, there's web.

We hadn't walked ten paces before our faces were covered in it: tickly, itchy and *freaky*. I properly freaked after two more steps. Managed to swallow it down for another one and then couldn't help screaming out, 'I can't do it!'

I clawed at my face and neck, desperate to get rid

of the cobwebs. There was no way I'd survive this. It felt like spiders were crawling everywhere. And if you've ever been sat on by an older brother or sister who's trying to get you with a fart, you'll know what it feels like to be suffocating in hot, steamy, stinking jungle.

For the second time that day I was glad to have a genius baby brother. Johnnie had the answer.

'Look, there's a ladder!' he said, examining an especially large tree. He picked at the bark, and, as if by magic, a moss-covered rope ladder came away from the trunk. The more he pulled, the more it revealed itself.

'Go up and see which way it is to the rockets,' he said with his usual bossiness. I raced up, not even remembering to be afraid of heights. I was just so desperate to get above the spider zone.

Thirty metres later, when I reached the canopy,

what I saw blew my mind. And there was even a zip line.

'Johnnie, you've got to get up here. I can see everything: the pyramid, the mansion, *everything*. And, you're not gonna believe it, but there's a way to get straight there.'

There was a pause, and then his little voice spoke. 'I can't, 'Liza. My leg, remember. And what about Myrty?'

I'd forgotten that because of his weak left leg Johnnie could only ever go up one rung of a ladder. It's why we'd never had bunk beds.

'Don't worry, little bro. I'll come and get you.'

For once I was the one with the answers and it felt **brilliant**. All I needed for this were strong legs, and after all these years of running away from stuff I had legs of steel.

I flew down the rope ladder and found Johnnie

and Myrt exactly where I'd left them. Together we wrestled Myrt into a rucksack, and then Johnnie climbed on my back. He clung on to me like a little monkey, and I could feel his smile on the back of my neck as I began to climb.

And then we were zip-lining. Straight for the mansion and the pyramid at the heart of the island. Straight for the rockets and the control centre – our only hope of turning back Mum and Dad's rocket. Myrt shut her eyes, but Johnnie and I kept them open for every wonderful second. We wanted to shout and scream, but knew we shouldn't. And, besides, it would have just set Myrt off.

From tree to tree we went. With each tree I needed to climb another ladder, ready for the next zip line. And tree by tree we crossed the rainforest.

It's funny to say it, but all the way up there in the canopy, working the zip lines with Johnnie, was one of best times of my life. You wouldn't believe the things we saw. Every tree was its own world of wonders.

GLASS FROG = BEST DAD IN THE WORLD?

Parasitic wasps try to lay eggs inside the frog eggs. So the baby wasps will get to eat the baby frogs! Gross. But Glass Frog Dad fights them off with Ninja Kicks!

Who will win?? Super-dad or the wasps?

Frog's eggs

GIANT MONTANE PITCHER PLANT = BEST LOO IN THE WORLD?

It's the world's biggest carnivorous plant. It's even big enough to eat a rat! But it prefers to eat poo??!
So it feeds Tree Shrews sweet, laxative nectar. The shrew licks this inside of its toilet, and bingo, it's gotta go.

Tree Shrew loo

BEE HUMMINGBIRD + HAWK = BEST FRIENDS IN THE WORLD?

The Bee Hummingbird is the world's smallest bird. In a fight with a crow it wouldn't stand a chance. BUT, it's got a secret weapon. A hawk = BEST FRIEND! The Hawk acts like the hummingbird's bodyguard and nobody knows why!! How cool is that???

All too soon we were at the edge of the jungle. We'd made it to the mansion at the heart of the island. The only way was down towards a manicured croquet lawn. The pyramid lay beyond, rising up from behind the massive house. That's how close we were to the rockets.

We waited in that last tree for a good ten minutes, scouting out the lie of the land. The house itself was huge, but the gardens were even bigger and laid out like something from Disneyland. There was a reverse helter-skelter, tennis courts and even a lazy river, a kind of moat with giant turtles drifting around in it. We fought over turns on Johnnie's telescope and in close up, things were even weirder. A robot lawnmower whirred away on the lawn. Nothing weird about that, except it had a little monkey sitting on it, chattering away as it pulled on the steering wheel. There were giant insects everywhere too, and a giraffe with a saddle.

We could have spent all day looking and wondering about the man who'd dreamed all this up. It was like he'd taken a little kid's drawing and turned it real. But the sun was shifting in the sky, and time was precious.

We had to make a move.

'As soon as we hit the ground, we run,' I said to Johnnie. 'Got it?'

He nodded. The only way to the pyramid, to the control centre, was to get round the house and into the jungle beyond.

With Johnnie clinging on to my back, and Myrt in the rucksack on my front, we zipped downwards for the last time. But as soon as my feet hit that lush green lawn, I knew we were in trouble. Big trouble.

The grass turned red as soon as I touched it. The actual grass. Waves of colour radiated out in a ripple across the lawn.

'What's it doing, Johnnie?'

I could feel Johnnie wriggling about on my back, struggling to see. But he never got the chance to answer. In seconds we were found by a pack of monkey-driven lawnmowers. There were five of them, blades humming, monkeys chattering. They closed in a circle until we were surrounded. I never did like monkeys.

They stopped, but only for a moment, and then the lawn changed again. It turned yellow, forming a strip towards the house, ending at some steps that led on to a terrace. The pack of mowers opened their circle so we could step on to the yellow path. It was pretty obvious what we were supposed to do.

Johnnie scrambled off my back and we got Myrt

out of the rucksack, and the three of us tentatively

stepped across the yellow strip of lawn and made

our way towards the mansion.

As we stepped into the shade of the terrace, a large head appeared from over the top of a tall newspaper. There'd been someone there the whole time, sitting at a table and hidden behind a thick screen of flowering bougainvillea. Suddenly the reality of what we'd done pulled us up short. We had broken into someone's mansion at the heart of a mystery island. An island not on any maps, and guarded by enough bizarre technology to suggest the owner had secrets. Secrets they didn't want to give up.

This was going to take some quick talking.

HOW TO TALK YOUR
WAY OUT OF TROUBLE

'How'd you do?' the head said. The small neat beard was familiar. So were the eyes. I should say, so was the EYE. The BIG EYE.

Myrt immediately went to bite him, but I grabbed her collar.

'You're Noah,' said Johnnie. 'The flying-taxi man.'

The beard smiled, and so did one of the eyes. The small one. 'Yipperdy-yep, that's me. Welcome to the island.'

We were beckoned forward towards his table. Noah gave us

another broad, beaming smile. 'Take a seat. You're the first guests I've ever had,' he said. 'Congrats.'

We sat, both smiling politely, not sure exactly what to say.

'No one, bring more lime soda.'

I looked at Johnnie, raising my eyebrows in a silent question.

But before Johnnie could respond, an ancient-looking robot wheeled itself up to the table. It pulled a jug of lime soda out from where its stomach should be. Noah looked delighted.

'Ha! Just ma li'l joke. He's number one, the first robot I ever made. Not bad for a nine-year-old kid, eh? He's had an upgrade or two obviously.'

We looked blank.

'Number one . . . no

one,' he said, drawing the letters in the air with his finger. 'D'ya get it?'

Everyone knows that if you have to explain a joke, it's not funny. But Johnnie managed to laugh, and Noah looked pleased. 'Nobody, bring ice.'

This time he couldn't hold back a snort as a flying ball buzzed out of the terrace doors carrying an ice bucket. It flew over and dropped the bucket on to the wooden table with a bang. Ice spilled, but Noah didn't seem to mind.

'Ha! No body, do you get it? It's just a head. *No body.*' He laughed as if he'd heard the joke for the first time. And then suddenly he stopped. 'Just a little joke. But you should probably know Nobody has a laser cannon. Best you wear these while you're on the island.' He fished three bracelets out of a pocket and slid them across the table. 'These will ID you as friend, not foe.'

I slipped one of the bracelets on and it compressed tight round my wrist. It flickered through every colour of the rainbow before settling on green. As it did, the flowers on the climbing plant started moving, flapping. And it was only then that I saw they weren't flowers at all. They were butterflies. Hundreds of them, fluttering away in all directions. One landed on the table right in front of Johnnie, a giant butterfly the size of a dinner plate.

'That's so cool,' said Johnnie, unable to take his eyes off it. 'Is it a robot?'

Noah reached out his finger and the butterfly hopped on. 'This robot cost a small fortune.'

'Did you use graphene[10]? For the wings?'

Noah smiled and nodded. 'You're a sharp one. Not bad for a preschooler.'

After that, the normal pattern of my life resumed. It was like I wasn't even there. All Noah wanted was to talk with genius Johnnie. I should have been grateful to avoid those freaky eyes, but I wasn't. Instead I had to stop Myrt chewing off the bracelet I'd put on her back leg. We both fidgeted irritably while Johnnie and Noah talked about making robots.

Eventually, after draining his glass, Noah changed the subject. 'Let's have luncheon, and you can tell me what you're doing on my island.'

Suddenly he didn't look quite so friendly. I looked at Johnnie but he was still mesmerized by the robot butterfly. It was obvious I was going

---

10 In case you know as much about graphene as I did – it's a form of carbon that's really thin. It's one atom thick.

to have to do all the talking.

'So,' he repeated, 'what *are* you doing on my island?'

I stared at him. All I knew at the time was that this was Mum and Dad's boss, the world's richest man. A man with a secret island and a big eye. And the big eye seemed to get bigger the longer he waited for me to answer his question.

I decided to tell him our story over lunch (who still calls it 'luncheon'?). It took time but I went right back to the beginning. I told the truth. Well, I left some bits out, loads of bits, but everything I said was true (does that still count as the truth?[11]).

For one thing, I didn't tell him that I was hoping to maybe steal one of his rockets. For another I didn't tell him Mum and Dad had been hacked. I'm not an idiot; you should never trust a man with one really

11 Editor's footnote: No.

147

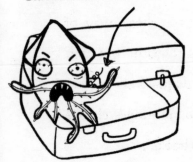

BRAIN INTERFACE NODE

big eye. And, besides, he had a robot with a laser cannon.

He seemed happy enough with what I was saying; he was nice. He was particularly interested in the vampire squid in Johnnie's lunchbox.

We opened it up, right there on the table, and sure enough, Johnnie's plan had worked. There was only one squid left, the alpha squid. It had eaten all the rest.

'Probably best shut the lid,' said Noah quietly, so I did. But you could hear the alpha squid's beak scraping against the inside of the plastic. It gave me the heebie-jeebies, so I put it back in Johnnie's backpack and zipped it shut.[12]

Johnnie broke the silence that followed. 'Did you

12 Don't judge. He was the one who wanted to keep it!

see the BIN? In the squid? It's a *biobot.*'

Noah nodded. 'There've been reports of illegal BINs coming out of Russia. It's a cheap way of building robots.' He scratched his beard. 'But why would they use them in vampire squid?'

'Mum and Dad have one too.' Johnnie's cheeks were pinking up. 'They've been hacked.'

I held my breath, half expecting Johnnie to accuse Noah of hacking Mum and Dad. Who knew what would happen then.

But he didn't. He just watched and waited as Noah looked at him. Neither one blinked.

'What makes you say that?' Noah turned to me, still not blinking.

'We saw them,' I said quietly but clearly. 'On my phone. If you zoom in, it's definitely a BIN.'

Noah's little eye finally blinked. And then he dropped his head into his hands with a look of despair. He sat like that for a while, head down. I looked across the table at Johnnie and made a face, as if to say, 'So what do we do now?'

Johnnie pulled an even bigger face and shook his head, as if to say, 'How'd I know?'

Thankfully the awkward silence didn't last too long.

Noah looked up. First at Johnnie, then at me. 'It's not the first time, you know.'

'What do you mean?' asked Johnnie.

'We've had problems like this before.' Noah turned to me, and his little eye suddenly looked tired. 'My first crew, both of them. Someone, some government probably, hacked them too.'

'So Mum and Dad weren't even the first choice?' I said it louder than I meant to.

'They weren't even second choice,' said Noah quietly. 'They were fifth choice.'

'Fifth?' I was really loud now but I didn't care. 'Fifth choice? What happened to all the others?'

Noah bit his lip. 'They were all hacked.' He stood and started pacing. 'I just don't understand; it's impossible. We were so careful.' He was pushing his hand through his hair, pulling at it. 'No one even knows where this island is.'

'But who would hack your astronauts?' I was suddenly angry. I wanted answers.

'Who wouldn't?' said Noah, scratching his palm. 'The Americans, the Chinese – every government in the world wants a piece of this.' He waved in the direction of the pyramid. 'We're the first manned mission to Mars. Do you know what that means?'

I shook my head. 'You get to put the flag in?'

He laughed but with no joy. 'The flag? You think I'm doing this for a flag?'

I kind of half nodded, half shook my head, not sure what to say.

'This is a whole new world. A brand-new planet, full of minerals and resources and space and *hope*. Whoever controls Mars, controls the future. Mars *is* the future.'

Eventually he seemed to make a decision. 'I think we can help each other,' he said simply. 'You wanna talk to your momma and poppa and see if they've really been hacked? Well, so do I. And if they have, we'll turn that spaceship right round.'

'You can do that? Turn the ship round? From here?'

'Why do you think the control room is called the control room?'

He nodded in the direction of the pyramid and I

made a mental note.

My heart skipped a beat. 'We can talk to them? But aren't they too far away?'

Noah laughed. 'Radio waves travel at the speed of light, li'l lady. How fast do you think they're going?'

It sounded like a trick question. I looked at Johnnie, but he was busy sucking on his double straw to get the last bit of melted ice and lime soda.

'*Less* than the speed of light, maybe?' I said, knowing that I was missing something.

'You betcha! Now, let me get things sorted out and you can talk the night away.'

No.1 returned to the table, somehow anticipating Noah's next sentence. 'No.1 will take you up to your rooms. I'll call you when everything's set up.'

I looked at Johnnie to see what he was making of all this. But he pulled a face that I didn't understand, and I couldn't ask in front of Noah.

Without needing to be asked No.1 wheeled over to the house and opened the double doors. Noah was up and through them without another word. He clearly expected us to follow.

'Do you trust him?' I whispered as soon as he was out of sight. But Johnnie was climbing down from his chair.

'Why not? What have we got to lose?' was all he said.

I wanted to argue it out, but he was already following Noah into the shade of the mansion.

HOW TO TRUST SOMEONE YOU DON'T TRUST

I'm not exactly sure what I was expecting inside the

house. But it certainly wasn't this:

Noah didn't break stride. 'Don't the mind the bonobobots,' he said, waving airily at the chimps. 'They're just robots.' He made his way to the far end of the hall. 'Just follow No.1 up them steps and I'll see y'all in a few hours.'

And with that Noah disappeared down into the basement, while we followed No.1 up to the first floor. Its robot tracks struggled with the stairs. Even Johnnie could keep up, but upstairs we became lost in a labyrinth of corridors. Eventually the robot stopped, turned and opened two doors. One on either side of the corridor.

'Please pick,' it said in a not-unfriendly robotic voice. 'Gaming Room or Chocolate Fountain Room?'

Johnnie chose the Gaming Room and I didn't argue. And I'm glad I didn't. I *definitely* got the best room. It totally had the best gadgets. And, besides, if we'd chosen the other way round, things would have turned out very different. I'd be a mindless zombie robot for one thing. But that was all to come. For now I was just blown away by the stuff I found in my room.

I GOT THE BEST ROOM (FOR ONCE)

MY ROOM:

CHOCOLATE FOUNTAIN ALARM CLOCK

PARAGLIDING SIMULATOR BED

CLIMBING WALL MADE OF SWEETS

AIR HAMMOCK (FAN-BASED HAMMOCK THAT BLOWS TO KEEP YOU OFF THE GROUND)

DOG BED IN THE SHAPE OF A DEAD CAT

JOHNNIE'S ROOM:

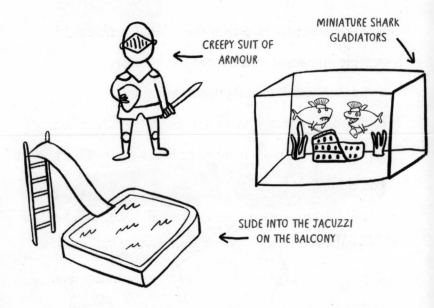

CREEPY SUIT OF ARMOUR

MINIATURE SHARK GLADIATORS

SLIDE INTO THE JACUZZI ON THE BALCONY

Tempting though it was, I didn't waste much time exploring. I waited a few minutes, to make sure No.1 had gone, and then stepped across the corridor to find Johnnie. If Noah thought he'd distract us with a few cool gadgets, he was very much mistaken.

Johnnie was already in a game, Myrt on his lap. They barely looked up, so I went to explore the balcony. It directly faced the pyramid.

'That's got to be where the control centre is,' I whispered back into the room.

Johnnie didn't say anything.

'The cross on the map, Johnnie, the cross at the top of the pyramid. It must be the way in. Don't you think?'

But Johnnie just wasn't interested. I yanked the controller out of his hand and he yelled. The little sharks in the fish tank all floated to the surface, like they'd just died.

What are you doing, Eliza?'

'What are *you* doing?' I repeated.

'I'm waiting. Like we said we would. Waiting for Noah to make contact with Mum and Dad.'

'You mean you trust him?' I said.

He bobbed his head, half nod, half shake. 'What choice do we have? What else are we going to do?'

Johnnie held out a hand; he wanted the

controller back.

I could feel my heart pumping in my chest. 'Fine, you stay here and play your stupid shark game.' I threw the controller at him.

But when I got to the door it was locked. If I hadn't trusted Noah before, I definitely didn't trust him now.

I immediately ran back out to the balcony: but we were three floors up, and there was nothing to climb on.

Two miserable hours went by with Johnnie playing and me pacing. It was only as the sun moved west and began to disappear behind the giant pyramid, that I realized how long we'd been trapped. I also realized something else: the whole house and lawn were turning so they always faced the sun.

I eventually prised Johnnie away from the game

and we both went on to the balcony for the sunset. In a flourish of reds and purples, the sun fell behind the pyramid and the sound of jungle cicadas filled the warm evening air.

Then came a knock on the door, and No.1 trundled in without waiting for an answer.

'Good evening, sir, madam. We have finally made contact with your parents. Mr Noah requests your presence in the Vlogging Studio.'

It paused but just for a moment, then wheeled back into the corridor. I looked at Johnnie and he nodded back, as if to say, 'Told you we should just wait.'

This was it, our big chance to remind Mum and Dad that they loved us. To persuade them to turn the rocket round and come back. And to find out, once and for all, if they really had been hacked.

It was time Mum and Dad started doing what *we* wanted.

HOW TO GET YOUR PARENTS TO DO WHAT YOU WANT

Some kids have actually been known to hypnotize their parents.[13] People at school say Sadie Snickpick's done it. And that's why she gets everything she wants. It must be brilliant if you can pull it off.

Other kids just use tears or a whiny voice to get their way. Controlling normal parents is surprisingly easy; there's a whole chapter of 'practical tips' in *The Book of Secrets* that tells you everything

---

13   It's my *favourite* chapter in the whole book: **Secret 19: How to Hypnotize Your Parents**. And this is the most useful chapter in the whole thing. Johnnie's copied out his favourite tips; see Appendix 1 at the back.

you need to know. But none of that was going to work for us. If our parents had been hacked, they were being controlled by somebody (somebody unknown, maybe the US government, maybe the Chinese, but my money was still on Noah) through the BINs in their brains. Getting them to do what we wanted was going to take a miracle.

As we followed No.1 down the giant stairway my mind raced with ideas. And I cursed the time Johnnie had wasted on the shark game. We should have been plotting and scheming. Maybe there was some way of talking to Dad's unhacked right brain.

I looked at Johnnie as we entered the great entrance hall. The bonobobots were still busy, tapping away at their computer terminals. God knows what they were doing. Johnnie looked stern. He was chewing his lip, always a bad sign. Myrt growled as we walked among the apes.

She wasn't happy either.

Then finally we went down another set of stairs and into the Vlogging Studio.

'*Hola, bienvenu* and welcome! Welcome to my Vlogging Studio.' Noah waved us in and towards a giant beanbag the size of a car. 'This is where I record my video blog. But we can use it to talk to your parents.'

There were cameras everywhere, and it was the size of a television studio. Not that I've ever been in a television studio.

Noah's vlog, I discovered later, was the most popular vlog in the history of vlogging. He had 691 million subscribers. But today, thank goodness, we were just going to be talking to Mum and Dad.

We sat down and stared at the huge 3D screen. Noah's company logo bounced around right in front of us.

'Sorry it took so long,' said Noah, his big eye looking unusually small for once. '*Red Rover* was in the shadow of the moon for longer than we anticipated.'

Johnnie saw the look of alarm on my face and reached out to reassure me. 'It just means the moon was blocking the signal.'

'OK, ready?' said Noah, nodding at No.1.

And, before we could answer, the screen came alive, and there, in three glorious dimensions, right in front us, life-size and so real you could almost touch them, were Mum and Dad.

I screamed and they smiled. And for a moment I

just knew everything was going to be all right.

And then they spoke, and I knew it totally wasn't.

'Hello, kiddos,' they said in suspiciously perfect unison. 'It's lovely to see you.'

Johnnie had jumped up from the beanbag. He reached out but his hand just passed right through them.

The 3D image pixelated, but just for a moment, and Noah interrupted to say, 'We think there's a meteor shower, so we might not have the signal for long.' He looked genuinely worried.

Johnnie reached out for my hand and said emphatically, 'Do you trust me?'

I nodded, and he turned to Noah.

'We need paper and a pen. And we need to get Dad to cover his right eye.'

This was more brain-science mumbo jumbo, but I trusted Johnnie's knowledge. And so when No.1

produced a pad of paper and a marker pen, I just sat
back and hugged Myrt. It was time to let Johnnie do
his thing.

'Dad, I need you to cover your right eye with
your right hand,' he said. 'Can you do that for me?'

Dad looked at Mum and then at Noah. But Noah
looked unsure. Eventually he nodded.

Dad covered his eye just as Johnnie had
instructed, and Johnnie wrote on the pad and
held it up.

Dad shifted in his chair and held up a hand.
Slowly he unfurled his fingers: one, then two, and
finally three.

'Is that true? Do you really want to come back?' asked Noah.

But this time Dad just shook his head.

Mum answered for him, 'No, this is the Chance of a Lifetime.'

And then, without warning, the feed went dead.

'They must have entered the meteor shower,' said Noah.

Then he turned to us and said the words I most wanted to hear in all the world.

'Something's not right. I'm turning that rocket round.'

'Really?' said Johnnie.

I couldn't even speak.

'Yes, really,' said Noah. 'We're aborting the mission.'

I turned to Johnnie and grabbed him. And we jumped up and down, hugging each other.

Myrt chewed my hand in all the excitement but I didn't care.

'If you'll excuse me,' said Noah, 'I need to get to the control room and initiate the recall.'

'Can we come?' I asked, but Noah shook his head.

'Leave it with me. I'll let you know as soon as they're on the new flight path. It may not be easy.'

I opened my mouth to object, but Noah held up a hand to silence me. 'Just be patient; you've done all you need to do. Now you just need to go to bed, get some sleep, and wait.'

He looked so sincere, so genuine. I just nodded.

Mum and Dad were coming home.

We just had to go to bed, get some sleep, and wait.

HOW TO WAIT

Back in Johnnie's bedroom we had a huge argument.

'Told you,' he said, smug as anything. 'Assume all will be well, and well it will be.'

It's what Dad says at school drop-off. And he's mostly wrong and always annoying.

'Dad says that every time he drops me off at school and it's *never* OK.'

'Eliza, relax! Mum and Dad are coming back; we've done it. Just enjoy it!'

'We don't know for sure; we've only got Noah's word.'

It went on like that, round and round in circles, until I got properly angry.

'You think you're so clever. You think you know everything, but you don't. *That's* why it's so hard to like you.'

Unable to look at Johnnie's face any longer I stormed out, slamming the door. Myrt followed me back to my room. At least she was on my side. It was late and we huddled up together and tried to sleep. But despite everything, despite the fact that I should have been happy and celebrating, sleep came slowly.

When it did come, I slept badly. The air was heavy and Myrt was busy. She kept waking me, pacing around in circles to get comfortable on the silky sheets. Thank the stars she did.

I heard it before I saw it. Something scratching across the floorboards, coming towards the bed.

Then it went quiet, and that was even worse.

I felt a weight tugging at my sheet and then

whatever it was, was up on the bed, wriggling over my legs towards my body.

I kicked in a panic and felt it flick up. For a moment it was silhouetted in the moonlight and then landed back down, right on my chest. I screamed but it just kept coming. I clawed with both hands, but it was stuck fast, it just wouldn't stop. And then it was in my hair and I could feel its mouth biting, trying to burrow into my head with the sound of a dentist's drill.

Then Myrt was on me too and I felt her teeth, searching and biting and suddenly the thing was off. I had the light on and saw it properly for the first time. Myrt had it pinned to the bed with both paws.

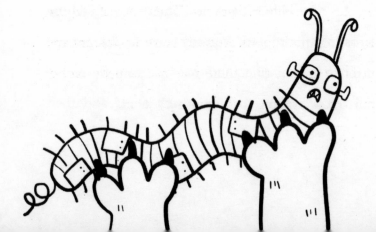

I found a trainer to use as a weapon, but before I could use it, Myrt's jaws had finished the job.

INSIDES OF A CENTIPEDE BIOBOT

It was a mix of goo and electronics, a biobot. And there, at the tail, hardly visible in the dim light, was an oh-so familiar coil of wire. Then I heard a squeal from Johnnie's room. And I knew, with instant and utter certainty, that there was a centipede biobot burrowing into my baby brother's head.

HOW TO STOP A CENTIPEDE BIOBOT BURROWING INTO YOUR BABY BROTHER'S HEAD

It's easy if you've got a Myrt.

It took her seconds and the bug was crunched. It took Johnnie longer to recover. A lot longer. He was sobbing like a little baby and I realized, perhaps stupidly late, that there was no longer a mum or a dad to cuddle him when he was sad or upset. There was just me.

We sat there hugging on Johnnie's bed in the dark. Eventually I held his cheeks in both hands and looked at him. 'Are you good?'

He nodded, and wiped away some tear-snot with the back of his hand.

'Johnnie, this is how he hacked Mum and Dad. This is how he gets the BINs into people's heads.'

We looked at the shattered centipede. The thought of it burrowing into Mum and Dad's brains made me feel sick.

'We still don't know it was him.'

'Johnnie!' I wanted to scream but I didn't. 'Of

course it was him. He's a monster. He's turned Mum and Dad into biobot zombies, and he's trying to do the same to us.'

Johnnie's head dropped.

'Face it, Johnster,' I said more softly, 'he's tricked us. Mum and Dad aren't coming back. We need help.'

I suddenly realized how hopeless everything was.

'But who? How?' Johnnie looked like he was about to start crying again.

And then I had my brainwave. At the time it seemed like the best idea ever.

'We ask 691 million people for help.'

Johnnie nodded, understanding immediately. We were going to broadcast on Noah's video blog.

'He won't dare do anything if the whole world knows we're here. We just need to tell them what he's up to.'

It was time to ask for help.

HOW TO ASK
FOR HELP

Asking for help is one of the hardest things people have to learn. And most of us never manage it. Think about the last time your dad's satnav went glitchy. Did he pull over and ask politely for directions? Or did he grumble and get flustered and spend ages shouting at his phone? Thought so.

But asking 691 million people for help was on a completely different scale. Imagine the biggest stadium in the world packed with people. Now imagine another one, and another, and then 6,898 more stadiums all just like it. *That's* 691 million people. But first we had to get down to the Vlogging Studio.

We didn't hang about. I grabbed our bags and we crept out into the corridor. I half expected to see Nobody standing guard, but it was empty. And dark.

Myrt's got an amazing sense of smell and she led the way, until eventually we made it to the big entrance hall. The bonobobots had shut down for the night, slumped over their computer terminals.

The quiet was eerie, but as we got close you could hear them softly breathing, their chests rising and falling gently with each breath. I could feel Myrt shaking as she pressed into my leg.

'They're biobots too,' said Johnnie, way too loud. If they woke now, we were dead.

In the moonlight I could see easily enough and we threaded our way through them desk by desk until we'd made it to the top of the basement stairs. And without looking back we were in the Vlogging Studio. Objective 1 complete.

'Who's doing the talking?' I asked nervously, but Johnnie didn't hesitate.

'I will,' he said in a blink. 'I'll do it.'

I took of breath of relief. The thought of talking to 691 million people left me feeling like the vampire squid in Johnnie's lunchbox was sucking on my stomach.

Sorting out the lights, cameras and everything took a while, and by the time we'd done it I'd figured out what Johnnie needed to say.

'Just tell them we're on Noah's island, that he's turned our mum and dad into biobot zombies and that we want our family back.'

'And the longitude and latitude, so they know where we are,' added Johnnie.

'Yeah, and we need to tell them it's urgent. Tell them we're in danger,' I finished. 'We should make some notes so you don't forget anything.'

It didn't take long. Soon we were all set. I gave Johnnie his notes, pressed a button and the camera light went green. A huge image of Johnnie came up on the screen and then this happened:

Johnnie got stage fright. With a sinking heart I realized it was down to me. If I wanted to save my family, I needed to forget the 691 million people, forget about what might go wrong, about every possible way I might make an idiot of myself. I took the notes from Johnnie's sweaty little hand, looked into the camera and filled my head with this thought:

Just read one word and then the next.

I read. Slowly at first. Then faster, until there were tears spilling down my cheeks and Johnnie was holding my hand and saying, 'Don't worry, 'Liza, it will be all right.' Myrt even jumped up on my lap and licked at my tears. But then I got to the final page and saw the words 'We don't have a mum or dad any more', and my throat went heavy and tight, and, try as I might, I just couldn't get my mouth to work. I looked at Johnnie. His chin was wobbling, but he still managed to squeeze my hand three times. And somehow that gave me the strength to finish.

'We don't have a mum or dad any more. They were forced on to that rocket. Please help us save our family.'

Then I pressed stop.

I looked at Johnnie. He was smiling. We'd done it.

181

'I'd like to see the look on Noah's face when he sees that!' I said, and Johnnie laughed.

And then we heard a cough from the top of the basement stairs. Noah was leaning over. His face was a mask of fury. His eye looked like it was about to explode out of his head.

'You'd better come up. It's pancakes for breakfast,' was all he said.

And despite everything, despite all the things I could have thought about, one picture filled my head: pancakes with sugar, lemon juice and exploded eyeball goo.

HOW TO EAT PANCAKES WITH EXPLODED EYEBALL GOO

Breakfast was awkward. But there was no eyeball goo.

The morning sun was up when we got to the terrace. Noah's face was back to a more normal colour and his eye no bigger than usual (which was still big but not explode-y big).

We sat down at the table and the silence seemed to go on for ages. It felt like the time I'd been called to the head's office because Sadie Snickpick had used a drone to dump her cabbage on my lunch plate, and I'd refused to eat it.

But this time there was a laser cannon hovering over our heads. And it didn't take long to realize our wristbands had changed from green to amber.

'I'm very, very disappointed in you.' Noah spoke through a mouthful of pancake, but it didn't make him look any less dangerous.

Myrt growled and I pulled her closer.

'Because you wanted to turn us into brainless zombie biobots but you couldn't?' said Johnnie.

'Shut up and eat your pancakes.' Anger flashed across Noah's face. 'I was UPGRADING you, you MORON.'

Despite everything, I ate some pancake. They were delicious and cinnamon-y. And it had the added advantage of keeping my mouth busy. I had a feeling Noah wanted to do all the talking.

'Humans are old tech. You're weak. You're not fit for the future. Without an upgrade you'd sit on your butts all day staring at screens.' His voice was getting louder again, and he showed no sign of slowing down.

'Endless, pointless games or worse: watching someone else gaming all day. As if gaming wasn't a big enough waste of life, you all want to watch other people wasting their lives. The whole human species needs an upgrade. I was giving you the chance to be better, and you threw it away you . . . you *idiots*!'

Noah was sweating through his shirt; something told me wasn't enjoying this either. He took some deep noisy breaths and then looked right at me. 'I *try* to do the right thing.'

'What? Stuffing that thing in our brains while we're asleep?'

Noah's big eye almost rolled out of its socket. 'Trust me, you won't enjoy that thing going in while you're still awake. It gets messy when you're awake.'

The thought of a centibot drilling its way into my skull made me swallow my mouthful of pancake without even chewing it.

'It's your fault, Eliza Lemon; remember that, it's *your fault*. I tried to do the right thing. I tried to make it easy. But, no, Little Miss Meddler had to make it difficult.'

'So it was all pretend?' Suddenly my hands were shaking. 'All the "Mr Nice Guy", calling Mum and Dad on the rocket and "turning the rocket round", that was all pretend? Just so you could turn us into zombies in our sleep? Just so you didn't have to see us scream and shout and get your hands dirty? Just so we wouldn't make a scene and you wouldn't have to admit that you're *the bad guy*?'

Noah breathed out another long chestful of air. He suddenly looked tired.

'Me? The bad guy? I'm the one saving the world. Do you know what happens to Earth if we just let humans go on destroying it? If we don't give ourselves a backup on Mars? Oh no, I'm not the bad guy. I'm the guy who's going to save this stupid planet. And if that means upgrading a few people along the way, then that's what I'll do.'

I looked at Johnnie. He was tucking into yet another pancake; you had to hand it to the kid, stuffing his face in the face of the disaster.

And then Myrt, who'd been trapped safely between my legs, wriggled free and I knew instantly from Noah's face what she'd done. Through the years she'd bitten enough people for me to know immediately. She'd bitten Noah on the leg.

He kicked her away and jumped back, tipping over the table. Pancakes, plates, maple syrup, centibot innards – it all went flying.

Myrt's wristband flashed red.

I didn't even think. A laser cannon shot out of No.1's body and I leapt forward, grabbing Myrt and wrapping my arms round her. My eyes were shut and my head was down, buried into Myrt's doggy fur.

I waited for what seemed likes ages. But nothing.

I uncurled and looked up to see Noah's face still twitching with rage.

'I'm *not* the bad guy,' he repeated. 'I'm upgrading you. That's all.'

He looked at me and his eye seemed to throb in its socket.

'But everyone knows we're here, you maniac.' I was feeling desperate, and it made me wild. 'You touch us and you're finished. We've told them *everything.'*

'Then you'd better get ready to *un*tell them.'

But as he said it, something made him hesitate. He looked into the distance, as if he was listening out for something. For a moment I thought I saw a flash of fear cross his face. No.1 inched closer; its laser cannon pointed straight at my face.

'Put them in the Chokey,' said Noah, 'and this time make sure the centibots finish the job.'

And without another word he stood and went into the house.

HOW TO SURVIVE A CHOKEY FULL OF CENTIBOTS

That, it turned out, was the end of breakfast. No more pancakes for us.

'The Chokey' wasn't as bad as it sounded, though: a one-storey treehouse in the garden that had a removable ladder. Getting Johnnie and Myrt and two rucksacks[14] up the ladder wasn't easy – I had to carry virtually everything. And as No.1 knocked the ladder away, on to the lawn, it didn't take a Johnnie to see that getting down would be impossible.

---

14 Why No.1 brought our rucksacks didn't make sense to me either. I mean, who locks someone up and then gives them loads of stuff to help them escape? Johnnie reckons it was just part of No.1's butler programming. Johnnie says artificial intelligence is still 'Not quite there yet'.

Our prison was a jail without walls or bars or locks.

Just six metres of air.

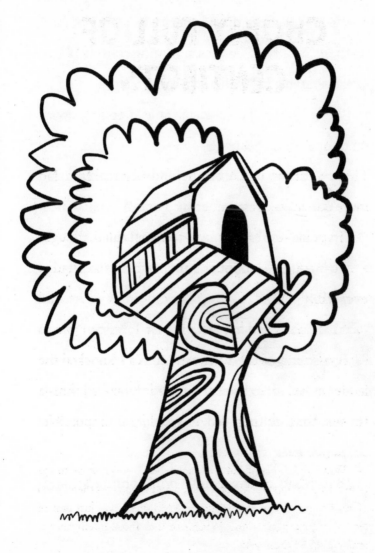

'So what now?' Johnnie said, as No.1 wheeled away.

We looked around, and there was plenty of stuff up there: beanbags, comics, a gaming console. There was even table football and a mini-fridge.

'We're gonna die,' said Johnnie, flopping down on to one of the beanbags.

'Don't say that. Come on, Johnst, we're not dead yet.' But I was remembering Noah's final words: 'Then you'd better get ready to *un*tell them.'

'He's going to biobot us and then get us to pretend everything's OK.'

'Yeah, so? We don't just give up, Johnster.'

The sound of the vampire squid's beak scraping away at the inside of Johnnie's lunchbox broke the silence that followed. A grim reminder of how desperate everything was.

'But what *are* we gonna do?' Johnnie's hands

were shaking, and he was shouting now. 'Fly out of here?'

I started to say something but before I could an idea exploded in my head.

I smiled. There in my imagination, but fully formed, was a picture of me, Johnnie and Myrt in a flying machine cobbled together from all the stuff we had up in the treehouse.

'Johnnie, that's it, you genius, we're gonna fly out of here.'

HOW TO
FLY

Flying, it turned out, isn't easy. It took ten million years for the first humans to get the hang of it. And then they all died in a terrible balloon crash. And *we* only had a pack of party balloons. I opened up our rucksacks on the treehouse floor.

'We've got all this stuff. We must be able to make some sort of flying machine,' I said purposefully. 'Let's draw up a list.'

And I did. And as I got it all down, I just knew that somewhere in that list was the answer to all our problems:

THINGS FOR MAKING A FLYING MACHINE

Beanbags x 3 (for crash landings?)

Game console (electricity!)

A tree (for making wings?)

Clothes (for rope?)

Table football (??)

Fridge full of mango juice and milk (?!)

First-aid kit- bandages, scissors

Pack of party balloons

Some seeds

A felt-tip

Head torch

World's Funniest Joke

The Book of Secrets

A dog (Myrt)

Alpha vampire squid in a lunchbox

Food and drink

ID bracelets

'OK,' I said, still full of confidence, 'we make wings out of leaves and branches and—'

'Won't work,' interrupted Johnnie, stuffing mango juice cartons and a milk bottle into his rucksack. 'Too heavy.'

But I wasn't going to be put off.

'Make a paraglider out of beanbag material?'

'It's cotton; the air goes straight through.'

'What if we chuck the beanbags out, and then jump down on to them? Not flying exactly but . . .'

Johnnie carefully looked out of the open treehouse door and pulled a face. 'You'd break your ankles. Besides, what are we going to do when we get down there? The lawnmower monkeys will be on to us, just like before.'

The hum of robomowers had already started for the day, and we both took a moment to look around. There were two mowers, each with a monkey on board, both loitering around the base of our tree.

'I think they're keeping guard,' said Johnnie, and he had a point. Noah had underestimated us once already; he wasn't likely to do it a second time.

I looked out of the open treehouse doorway, desperately searching for an idea. The gardens were so beautiful. Not the sort of place where you'd expect to be turned into a biobot zombie at all: the reverse helter-skelter[15], the lazy river with real turtles, and all the other animals: the giraffes and zebra and ostriches all saddled up and ready to race.

'What about if we tie the beanbags to our butts and jump that way?' I suggested.

'We break our butts instead of our ankles.'

His negativity was really beginning to bug me.

'So what *do* we do?'

---

15   Not that I like slides much, but an upwards slide!

But Johnnie was still fiddling with the games console. He nodded towards the mini-fridge. Through the glass door you could see it was full of mango cartons and little bottles of milk. 'Can I have a mango milkshake?'

I ignored that. 'Johnnie, Noah's coming back with more centibot things, and we'd better not be here when—'

I never finished my sentence, because the screen suddenly sprang into life. Not a game, but a TV news channel.

I watched in a blur of hope and amazement.

Because the news was hopeful.

And amazing.

THE NEWS WAS HOPEFUL AND AMAZING

It could only have been two hours since we'd made our broadcast, but the news had spread. Like wildfire.

The amazing thing was seeing me, Johnnie and Myrt on TV. On every news channel on the planet.

After that there was an interview with an angry-looking American general or admiral or somebody. He was saying things like 'It's time Noah was brought to heel' and 'The US military are ready to intervene'. And then it was back to us, so I made Johnnie turn it off.

I turned to Johnnie and he smiled back at me. 'Did you hear that general, Eliza? Noah must be pooing his pants.'

But now the screen was blank; it all seemed way too little, way too late.

Panic rose up from my stomach like acid. I felt sick. Like you do when you've messed up and you know it's too late to put things right.

'Johnnie, we're all out of time. Can't you see that?'

And then I heard the unmistakable sound of No.1 trundling back across the lawn. We watched him through gaps in the planks of the wooden treehouse. First through the wall and then through the floor as the robot arrived at the base of the tree. I held my breath and saw its metal body open, releasing a red beach ball on to the lawn.

It landed with a thud, and sat there, but only for a moment. Shimmering in the morning sun, I saw the ball shudder into life. And even from the top of that tree I could see exactly what it was.

A ball of centipedes.

A wriggling, writhing, living mass of centipedes.

Hundreds of them.

'Centibots!' shouted Johnnie in a failed whisper.

Myrt went wild, barking and growling and crashing around in a tight circle of terror.

Then the centibots began to unravel from the ball. And one by one they began to climb.

HOW TO ESCAPE FROM A CENTIBOT BEACH BALL

The centibots were climbing at a terrible speed. It was like the whole tree trunk was alive with them.

I started throwing stuff, trying to knock them off, but it was hopeless. The comic books just bounced off them. We tried heavier stuff, like the gaming console and some bits of tree, but even that did nothing. Their grippy little legs were like claws biting into the tree trunk. And, besides, most of what we threw missed completely.

I was about to chuck Johnnie's *Book of Secrets* when he grabbed my arm. 'No, Eliza.'

I turned, and his face said everything. It was all over. The steady crunch of centibot legs biting into the wood was getting louder the closer they got. They were over halfway. It wouldn't be long now. Myrt was barking uncontrollably, but even she couldn't crunch through a hundred centibots. One way or another they'd get into our skulls and then our brains and then who knows what it would be like. You can't ask a zombie what's it like to be a zombie.[16]

Tears streamed down Johnnie's face, and I pressed my sleeve on to his cheeks to dry them.

'I'll get your mango milkshake, Johnster,' I said softly, trying to smile. 'We've earned a bit of sugar.'

Sucking on some mango milkshake would at least dull the pain.

---

16 Actually you can. It's just you won't get a sensible answer. J xx

The crunching was so loud now it was like a car on gravel. I reached down into the fridge and poked the little straw into the mango carton. I even started wondering how to mix the juice with the milk to make a milkshake.[17] And then, like a gift from the imagination gods, I saw the answer.

I literally *saw* the answer.

Right there in my head.

The best idea of my life.

An idea so doubly genius that even I didn't know how good it was. Even after I'd had it. The words seemed to have been echoing around my head long before I said them: 'Everybody loves mango.'

I shoved Johnnie out of the way and slid on my front to the open door. The centibots were close and climbing, but I didn't miss a beat. I sprayed the mango juice right at them.

And, just like my brain had imagined,

---

17 Yeah, it's easy when you're not about to be zombified: drink both and then sloosh them about in your mouth. But at the time I had a lot to think about.

they stopped.

And turned.

And began to eat mango.

And, as they got covered in mango, they began to eat each other.

'More mango, Johnnie!'

I practically screamed and he jumped into action. Johnnie can't run much but he can throw. He chucked cartons across to me and I got spraying. The odd one got through, but Myrt was on to them in flash.

'Everybody *loves MANGO*!' screamed Johnnie, still chucking cartons at me. He was wild now, and, despite everything, I was laughing. There was mango everywhere and Myrt was gnashing in an orange-fuelled rage. The centibots didn't stand a chance.

'Mangooooo!!' Johnnie threw a wild carton

that went sailing over me. And I turned to see a giant head suddenly appear in the doorway of the treehouse. The head of a monster. It had huge eyes and horns and a long tongue that snaked out and started licking at the mango on the floor.

And then I realized why I didn't recognize what it was.

Giraffes' heads are *way* bigger than you think.

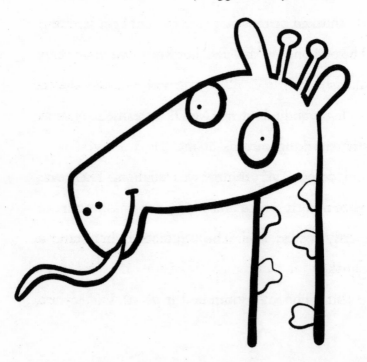

HOW TO RIDE
A GIRAFFE

Its head was the size of Johnnie. No kidding. And the tongue! Just the tongue on its own was as long as my leg.

You probably think that's an exaggeration because you've seen one at the zoo. But it's not. At the zoo giraffe heads seem small because they're a long way up. But up close they're huge. And we were up really close.

It probed for mango with a terrifying tongue, its huge mouth gaping wide.

Myrt went to bite it, but I grabbed her. Johnnie chucked another mango carton into its open mouth. The jaws chomped it down in one bite, carton, straw, everything.

And then I saw more centibots. They were creeping in from everywhere now. Through the cracks in the floor and the walls, dozens of them.

I looked at Johnnie clutching his rucksack like a shield, more terrified even than me.

And I knew exactly what I needed to do. The giraffe was our escape. We just had to get on without dying first.

Myrt was wriggling against my grip, but I held tight, and ran, dragging Johnnie and virtually throwing him over that horned head. Then I jumped myself. Trusting in heroes' luck as we slid down its thick mane.

It smells like a cow, I remember thinking, as I slammed into the saddle.

And then it went berserk.

It bellowed like it had been shot and immediately

broke into a gallop. It ran straight and it didn't stop, crossing the lawn in about ten seconds, clearing the lazy river without even breaking stride. How we held on for so long is a mystery. We crashed into the rainforest, its huge body breaking branches as it smashed a path through the jungle.

I held on for as long as I could, but it was like falling through an endless hedge. And then we were out into a clearing, and the pyramid was right ahead.

The giraffe swerved and fell. It literally fell over. And I was flung sideways, thumping down on to my back. Myrt landed on my chest, and I lay there, unable to breathe, gasping for air, as the giraffe got back to its feet with a bellow and disappeared into the jungle.

I could hear it over the sound of my own desperate gulps for air, smashing onwards, but getting quieter and quieter the further it went. And I could see blue sky and a cloud in the shape of a centipede. And then Johnnie's face was looking down at me.

'We've got to keep going.' He held up his wrist. The ID bracelet was flashing red. Mine was too, and Myrt's.

She'd been trying to chew hers off ever since I'd put it on. But I'd always managed to stop her. Until now. I ripped mine off with my teeth and the rubber tore surprisingly easily. Johnnie's baby teeth struggled, but I soon had three red-flashing bracelets in my hand.

I chucked them as far as I could, which wasn't far, and we ran to the pyramid, with Johnnie struggling to keep up.

There was a huge door; I hadn't expected that. Like a triple garage door and double the height. But there was no way in. I tried banging, but it just echoed back like a giant drum. And, besides, we knew what we had to do.

'We've got to go up,' I said.

Johnnie nodded. 'X marks the spot.' Then he piggy-backed on me.

The steps were big and it took all my muscle power to climb them. Myrt can jump on to the kitchen table when she wants to, but even she struggled. She managed it, though, jumping step by step, which was just as well, because I don't think I could have carried her. Not all the way up.

It took time, but we did it. And as the sun rose towards noon, we reached the top.

The view from up there was amazing.

'A battleship?!' said Johnnie, reaching for his telescope. 'And look, attack copters!'

But Noah's island was not without its defences.

We'd only broadcast three hours before. Things had gone very wrong for Noah. And they were about to get worse.

The first missile struck. We never knew which copter fired it, and it hit well wide, whining through the air before lighting up a huge patch of rainforest.

'They're not messing about,' said Johnnie.

And I knew then we had to act. We couldn't just sit there and wait to be rescued. Whatever general or admiral had ordered the attack was more interested in getting Noah than he was in helping us. Let alone Mum and Dad.

'What do we do?' said Johnnie, echoing the thought bouncing around in my brain.

Getting to the top of the pyramid hadn't solved anything. We'd followed Dad's instructions, we'd gone to the X marks the spot, and . . . nothing. There was nothing there, just a black-painted X and hole where it crossed.

'Don't ask me.' I was getting flustered. 'It's your stupid map.'

Johnnie pulled out the map and we both took another look.

'Look at the little arrow.' I felt my cheeks burn red.
'Go *down* here.'

Then the second missile struck. This one was closer. Too close. It made the pyramid shake as it gouged a huge crater into Noah's perfect lawn.

I knelt down to look at the hole in the centre of the cross. It was no bigger than my waist. Despite the midday sun, the inside was totally black. I stuck my head in and shouted, testing for an echo, and my voice came back in waves. Whatever was inside, the space below was huge. Another missile came zipping through the air. This one was intercepted by the laser, and it exploded harmlessly somewhere over the sea.

I saw three more missiles fire, and I suddenly knew what we needed to do: a leap into the dark. If we trusted Dad, we had to jump into that black hole. I thought about Dad, about all the fun we used to have. When I was young, he always had a million ideas for games and things to do. And no matter what we did, I was always safe. I could always trust him to keep me safe.

But did I trust him now?

HOW TO TRUST SOMEONE

'Johnnie, you need to jump first.'

Johnnie looked down into the hole and then up at me like I was some sort of crazy. 'No way, Eliza.'

'Johnnie, this is what's the map's telling us to do. This is what *Dad's* telling us to do. We have to trust him.' I held Johnnie's cheeks in my hands, like Mum used to do. 'We have to jump.'

'You jump, then,' said Johnnie, shaking his cheeks free.

'No. If I go, then you'll be stuck up here alone.' I took the head torch out of his rucksack and stuck it on his head.

'You remember what Dad taught you to say

when you're scared?'

'What do you mean? Scared but doing i—'

I never let him finish. One little shove and Johnnie was falling backwards into the black hole. I heard his scream and saw big eyes and then the light of his head torch disappearing into the void.

And then nothing.

Myrt looked down, sniffing the air, but even she could only sense empty space. And then we heard a voice from far below. Johnnie's voice.

'You've *got* to try that, 'Liza. Come on, jump. It's amazing.' It didn't take the seventh missile to persuade me. I knew in that instant that I trusted my baby bro completely. I grabbed Myrt, and two seconds later we were falling through black empty space – Myrt clawing, scrambling on to my shoulders and scratching my face as we fell.

And then we hit brick. Sponge bricks that broke our fall. Sponge bricks like the ones at soft play that I could remember from before Johnnie was born. You almost had to swim through them to get to the side. But it wasn't long before I'd climbed out of the sponge pit and joined Johnnie on the floor of the pyramid. Lights came on automatically, and of the things we saw and found on that island what we saw inside the pyramid was perhaps the most gobsmackingly gruesome of all.

The four walls were filled by row after row of containers, with every possible creature you could imagine. All frozen in suspended animation.

It was like some sort of nightmare zoo.

A zoo of death.

Some animals had tubes going in and out. There was a stunned-looking koala with a tube stuck in its rear. Others, like a giant spider crab, just floated about in a tank of green liquid. Some looked like they'd had all the water sucked out of them and been shrunk to a crisp. And if you looked carefully, they all had a bit of wire coming out of their heads. They were biobots. All of them.

But before we'd had time to take everything in, Noah's convertible came blasting through the doors

at the base of the pyramid. It landed with a bang and a skid.

I grabbed Johnnie and pulled him towards me. Noah was out of his car before it had even fully stopped. And his face told me we were in trouble.

'Well done, you, Eliza Lemon – you're not as stupid as you look.' Noah's voice was strangely metallic. Both eyes were smiling but cold, like he'd died in the middle of a joke.

Johnnie clung to my arm. Myrt took an angry step forward.

'Are these all biobots?' I looked up at the creatures, afraid of what I might see.

'This?' Noah waved a hand in the direction of his weird zoo walls. '*This* is my ark.'

'But what's it for?'

Another silly question, but I felt we'd be safe as long as he was talking. And the longer he talked, the longer Johnnie would have to come up with a plan.

'Isn't it obvious? *This* is the future.'

He talked for a bit then, about climate change and the End-of-Human-Civilization-As-We-Know-It and how humans are idiots. It was obviously a favourite subject.

The narwhal that you found? It was supposed to be part of my ark!

Do you know how much plastic there is in the stomach of a blue whale?

We dump a truck-load of plastic in the oceans every minute!

A garbage patch in the Pacific that's twice the size of America! Why all the vampire squid?? It's the acid, idiots!

We're the vampires – sucking the planet dry. The Earth's doomed. Get ready for Armageddon! But Mars will be mine!

Half of all species are going to be wiped out in the next twenty years! Do you know why?? Too many stupid people!

He talked for minutes. The trouble was, I knew it was true. I felt my head throbbing at the thought of it all. Our planet was doomed.

I gripped Johnnie's hand behind my back and squeezed it three times. If Johnnie was going to come up with a plan, now was the time to do it.

And then Johnnie screamed. As if something had bitten him on the back of the neck.

Which it had.

'Eliza! Get it off!'

The alpha vampire squid had finally eaten its way through Johnnie's lunchbox. And it was looking for fresh blood.

HOW TO ESCAPE FROM AN ALPHA VAMPIRE SQUID AND A MANIAC BILLIONAIRE ARMAGEDDONIST (AT THE SAME TIME)

It's obvious, really, when you've got time to think it all through afterwards over a cup of hot chocolate and a marshmallow: chuck the squid at the maniac and run.

We got there mainly through luck:

We ran to the rocket; it was the obvious place to hide. And we were up and in before Noah was even able to get the creature off his face. The last thing I saw, as I pulled shut the rocket door, was him jamming the squid into some piece of lab equipment.

The rocket was surprisingly small inside. Johnnie was already buckling himself into a safety harness.

'Come on,' he said, 'you wanted to steal a rocket.'

HOW TO STEAL
A ROCKET

It turns out that once you're in, stealing a rocket is easy. There are no keys. It's not like a car. No one who owns a rocket is expecting it to be stolen.

In fact, it didn't exactly need Johnnie Genius to figure out how to get the thing started.

The hardest bit was putting our safety harnesses on.

I held on to Myrt with both hands and Johnnie pressed the button. No countdown, no ignition sequence, just a fired-up booster engine and lift-off. The noise was unbelievable. I could see Myrt howling her little

heart out, but I couldn't hear her.

Screens sparked to life, cameras in every direction.

One showed Noah looking at us with his big eye. He had a red welt on the side of his face, and at first I expected him to shake his fist or shout. But he just smiled and nodded, almost as if everything was going to plan.

It was only then, as things started moving, that I remembered the pyramid roof. We'd been standing up there only a few minutes before, on thick, solid metal. The circle we'd jumped through was shining like a halo on one of the screens.

It was tiny.

I pictured the impact as we smacked into it, and the fireball of rocket fuel scorching us to death.

I looked up to tell Johnnie, but he was grinning too hard to listen.

Then, just as I began to scream, the circle began

to expand. And the top of the pyramid opened up like a flower bud.

I buried my head into Myrt's doggy fur, and shut my eyes.

Then Johnnie screamed and I jerked my head back up. His face was juddering with the vibrations of the rocket, and the noise was unbearable, but nothing could shake that grin off his face. I heard every word he said, but none of it made sense.

'We're going 74,000 miles per hour per hour!'[18]

18 I had to look that up afterwards. '74,000 miles per hour per hour,' means that *every* hour, you go *another* 74,000 miles per hour faster.

 And on the screen everything was getting small. The pyramid, the island, the ocean. Everything.

I looked at Johnnie, still juddering, still grinning.

And eight minutes later, the Earth was a blue ball floating in space.

We were in space.

In a rocket.

In outer space.

All we had to do now was steer it.

HOW TO STEER
A ROCKET

It's not like there's a steering wheel. On the plus side, it seemed to be programmed to go somewhere. One of the screens showed a map of the solar system with a flight path marked on. We'd hit the jackpot. There were no words, but the screen made it pretty obvious.

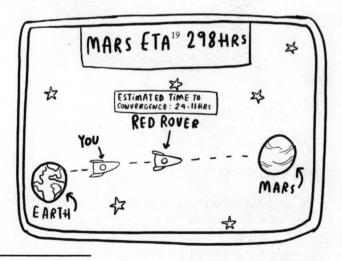

---

19 Estimated time of arrival.

The rocket was programmed for Mars, and it was set to converge with the flight path of the *Red Rover*. We were headed for Mum and Dad. Somehow, we were set to catch up with them in just over a day.

Johnnie's grin was so big it was off his face. And then I let go of Myrt. And she floated *upwards*. And Johnnie's grin got bigger.

We were in zero gravity.

And then we unbuckled our seat belts and just went *wild*. If you ever get a chance to go into outer space, **do it**. You will *never* have more fun.

The fun only stopped when:

It was lucky Myrt was hungry.[20]

Now this took pretty much the next few hours. And then we had to figure everything out like we were babies again.

And a million other things. We tried to radio Mum and Dad, of course, but even Johnnie couldn't get through to them. My phone was finally out of juice,[21] so that was no good, but it didn't matter, because every minute took us closer to them.

That night I should have slept with a warm

---

20 If you think that's gross, you should have been there when Johnnie was potty training on holiday once. I didn't kiss Myrt for a month.

21 Do phones even work in outer space? Johnnie would know.

No, of course not. J x

HOW TO EAT?

THE ANSWER IS
TEAMWORK

HOW TO SLEEP?

THE ANSWER IS
TEAMWORK

HOW TO GO TO THE LOO?

TEAMWORK CAN ONLY
TAKE YOU SO FAR

happy glow, but I barely slept a wink. When your pillow is never where you left it and Myrt's tail keeps slapping you in the face, sleep doesn't come easily. And, besides, the closer we got, the bigger my hopes. And the bigger my hopes, the bigger my worry.

And, sure enough, when we finally woke and put the TV on, we were brought right back down to Earth[22]. Johnnie flicked straight to the news. And the news was bad, very bad.

---

22 *Metaphorically not literally, J xx*

THE NEWS WAS
VERY BAD

It only took a moment, even for me, to work everything out.

'So Noah is going to colonize Mars? He's taking two of everything, and Mum and Dad are his two humans. All because he thinks the world is doomed?'

I didn't really expect an answer from either Johnnie or Myrt. But at the back of my mind was a more pressing question. 'Can he catch us up?'

'Probably not,' answered Johnnie, before I'd even asked the question. 'That pyramid's a terrible shape for going fast.'

But it wasn't long before we had a second opinion. Noah's big eye popped up on one of the screens and we saw him tapping a microphone. 'You should probably know, kids, I'm on precisely the same flight path as you. And, by No.1's reckoning, I should catch you up just after elevenses.'

Johnnie's face flushed pink; I could tell he was worried. 'Get lost, you big . . . *eyeball*.'

Noah laughed and held something up to the screen.

'Do you know what this is, Eliza Lemon?'

I looked at Johnnie and he shrugged. If he didn't know, I wasn't going to make a fool of myself guessing.

'This is the vampire squid you threw at me. I've sucked it dry, but it's only dormant, waiting for me to *re*hydrate it on your *FACE*!'

Johnnie was furious. I'd never seen his 'fierce face' look anything like it. 'Leave my sister alone! Or I'm going to . . .'

The discussion was going nowhere, so I hit the off switch before Johnnie could finish.

I looked at his tear-streaked face. 'What time is elevenses?' I asked without engaging my brain.

Johnnie, bless him, answered in a way that didn't make me feel stupid. 'In about five hours.'

I looked back at the screen showing our flight path, and touched the *Red Rover* symbol, as if somehow, I was reaching out to touch Mum and Dad. But the screen flashed coldly. Noah would catch us in five hours, twenty-one minutes before we reached Mum and Dad.

From somewhere we needed extra speed.

'Well,' said Johnnie, trying to sound upbeat, 'I guess we'll just have to think of something really clever.'

'Don't worry, Johnnie,' I said with an unconvincing smile. 'I've never lost a space race yet.'

HOW TO WIN A SPACE RACE

The answer, unfortunately, is to be in the bigger ship with lots of thrust.[23] Massive pyramid space arks with engines on each corner, it turns out, go really fast.

We spent our first morning in space racking our brains for every possible way to speed up our rocket. We bashed buttons, pulled levers, we tried everything.

GO!

WE BASHED SOME BUTTONS

WE NEVER DID FIGURE OUT WHAT THE LEVER DID

---

23 *Actually, it all depends on the ratio of mass to thrust. SEE SECRET 102: HOW TO WIN A SPACE RACE J x*

And by the end of the morning, maybe because of all the weight we'd ditched, we'd knocked almost an hour off our Estimated Time of Convergence with *Red Rover*.

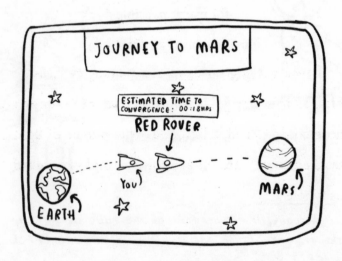

That extra speed should have been enough, but we were still eighteen minutes away when Johnnie let out a cry of despair. The rear rocket cam showed the image we'd been dreading.

OMINOUSLY CLOSING IN

It was gaining on us at a terrifying rate, point first, as if it was going to skewer us. But then the nose cone opened, a luminous blue bubble of light reached out towards us and the pyramid swallowed us whole.

We could hear our rocket being tethered, but I didn't dare look out. I glanced at Johnnie, but he was sucking his thumb. A really bad sign. Then Noah's grinning face was up on one of the screens, an even worse sign.

'Open up and say "Noooo! Ahhhhhhhh"!' he screamed in a fake kiddie voice, as our rocket door opened all by itself.

The rocket steps folded out automatically, clunk by clunk, and there, right below, stood a triumphant Noah. Nobody hovered above his right shoulder, laser cannon out.

We were well and truly stuffed. Noah wanted revenge, and this time *he* was holding the alpha vampire squid.

HOW TO ESCAPE FROM A MANIAC BILLIONAIRE ARMAGEDDONIST
WHEN HE'S HOLDING THE ALPHA VAMPIRE SQUID

When you're a million miles from Earth, facing a laser-wielding robot and a maniac holding a dehydrated alpha vampire squid, the best option is usually to keep your mouth shut and do as you're told. Somehow the pyramid had its own very weak gravity, and we tentatively bounced down the steps of our rocket.

Fortunately Noah sent Nobody back into the rocket to 'sort things out', and that evened up the odds a bit. Unfortunately he seemed to know what he was doing. The car from before was now anchored to the floor, and Noah sat on it, casually propped against the bonnet.

'I'm going to enjoy this, Eliza,' he said, absently picking at the scab forming on his cheek. 'You're going to be the finest addition to my army of biobots.'

With minimal effort he leapt two metres into the air, grabbing a handle on one of the animal containers on the wall. He held on with ease, typed something into the keypad, and we all watched wide-eyed as a centibot drifted out.

Myrt growled, recognizing it from before, but this one was different; it had little wings.

'A special adaptation,' said Noah. 'It's a cross between a centipede and a butterfly. Perfect for low-gravity living.'

CENTIBUTTBOT?

He gave it a shove and it drifted straight towards me, somehow using its creepy little bug legs to steer. I could already imagine it burrowing into my head. Johnnie squeezed my hand, but there was nothing he could do. It just came closer and closer, slowly wafting towards me, homing in on my neck. The horror was indescribable. I've only felt like that once before, in PE when Sadie Snickpick smacked me between the eyes with a hockey ball.

I just froze. There was nothing to stop it drilling into my skull and brain and turning me into one of Noah's biobots. Just like Mum and Dad. We were all doomed to be biobots for ever, unless I could do something, but I couldn't. I couldn't move an inch.

Then Myrt growled, and jumped, and rose, and snapped. And the bug was gone, crushed between her jaws.

'Ha!' said Johnnie. 'Dog beats freaky centipede.'

But Noah's smile was rigid. 'Dog might beat centipede . . . but cobra beats dog.'

Another keypad, more tapping, and out came a snake. It bounced off the floor with a gentle bump, writhing as if in pain. Then it reared up, and came at Myrt like a lightning strike.

If you've only ever seen a snake sleeping, you're probably not afraid of them yet. But when a cobra rears up, jaws open, fangs dripping with venom, there's nothing much scarier.

Myrt let out a howl of fear, and she leapt and pawed at the air, but it was useless. The cobra came on.

Johnnie screamed like an animal and launched himself forward.

'But mongoose beats cobra!' he screeched, and I immediately knew what was going on in that brilliant little brain. He'd seen and memorized the code number Noah had used to release the snake and the flying centipede. And his encyclopaedic memory told him exactly which animal was needed to take on a cobra, which had evolved over thousands of years into the ultimate cobra-killing machine. There on the far wall, three metres up, a little plaque read *mongoose* – and with bounding steps Johnnie ran towards it.

But then his weak leg faltered. And he started veering to the left, and by the time he crashed into the wall he'd gone so far off course that he was stuck somewhere between a quetzal and a tapir.

Myrt was still flapping in mid-air, having made another leap to escape. Her eyes were wide in terror and the cobra was lunging, but neither could move fluently with such feeble gravity.

'Eliza, quetzal or tapir?' shouted Johnnie.

My mind was immediately blank. *The Book of Secrets* had a whole 'Who Would Win?' appendix at the back and Johnnie knew it off by heart. Bear vs tiger? Cheetah vs kangaroo? Chicken vs rabbit? He knew them all, every match-up in the animal kingdom. Why was he asking me?

But I only had to look at his face to know the answer. Johnnie's brain had seized up in panic.

'Just pick one!' he screamed, eyes fixed on the

keypads in each hand. 'Tapir or quetzal?!'

So I chose.

Life is the choices you make. And I chose 'quetzal'.

I know. With the benefit of hindsight that looks like a dumb decision. But sometimes dumb is dumb luck.

'Quetzal chokes cobra!' screamed Johnnie triumphantly.

But not for long.

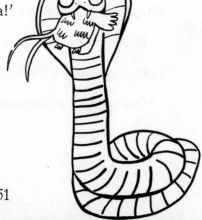

Noah lunged upwards, towards Johnnie, and grabbed him by an ankle, waving him about like a balloon as Johnnie desperately tried to cling on.

'Man beats preschooler,' Noah taunted with a laugh.

And then Nobody was out of the rocket, its laser pointed at my chest.

Our fight-back was over.

With very little difficulty Noah managed to stuff Johnnie into the boot of the car.

Johnnie is terrified of tight spaces, but with a laser cannon in my face there was nothing I could do. Myrt tried to help; she snarled and snapped but she just wasn't very good at moving in such feeble gravity. Soon No.1 had her bundled in the boot too.

Noah pulled a flat plastic box out of his pocket.

'Recognize this?' he asked, clicking open the box. The thing inside needed no describing. It was crisp-thin and looked dead, but I recognized it immediately. It was a vampire squid. *The* vampire squid. Noah grinned and tossed it into the boot.

'When that rehydrates, things should get interesting.' And he slammed the boot shut.

It was all down to me.

We were doomed.

My little baby brother had sacrificed himself for nothing and just the thought made me want to cry. But there wasn't even time for that.

HOPE = A BIG FAT ZERO %

Noah's face was an angry red, and I sensed we'd given him a scare. But that was all. I was surrounded, the situation was hopeless. Brainless-Zombie-Doom was my future. Was Johnnie's future. My family's future.

Compared to that, death would be a good result, I remember thinking. And it doesn't get any bleaker than that.

I've said before that sometimes it takes losing all hope to lose your fear. And something like that happened now. My imagination seemed to accelerate to a thousand thoughts per second. And with a smile I suddenly had a plan.

I knew exactly how to escape from Noah and his biobot zoo of zombie doom.

HOW TO ESCAPE FROM A MANIAC BILLIONAIRE ARMAGEDDONIST AND HIS BIOBOT ZOO OF ZOMBIE DOOM

I just had to act like a teenager.

When teenagers act like teenagers, adults find it annoying. But when younger kids do it, it drives them *absolutely insane*. Try it next time you're bored.

'You're such a loser.' I tried to look stroppy, like

my big cousin Olive. 'You do know they're gonna get you.'

'Shut it, you little *gump*.' Noah was swiping at the control panel. 'We catch *Red Rover* in five minutes. That should be plenty of time to prepare another centibot.'

I just ignored him. 'They're gonna kill you and you're such a stupid loser, you don't even know it.'

Noah looked up, and locked his big eye on to mine.

'They can kill you any time they like, loser,' I said with as much teenage sneer as I could muster.

'Nobody can kill me,' snapped Noah, and he emphasized every syllable.

Bingo.

I just smiled. And for two delicious seconds I could see Noah's brain trying to work out what I'd done. He was mouthing the words that he'd just said out loud, 'Nobody can kill me.'

The 'friend or foe' bracelet on Noah's wrist flashed through the rainbow, before settling on red.

He looked at the bracelet, and then at me, and for the first time I saw fear in those mismatched eyes.

Nobody's laser cannon rotated in an instant.

It fired, but Noah was too fast, ducking down as the laser blasted into the control panel behind him. But already Noah's quick fingers were reprogramming his bracelet.

I'd bought us seconds, but no more than that. With a lunge I got to the car and pulled myself into the driver's seat. I had to get away. Anywhere was better than this. But the car was somehow docked to the floor. There was an old-fashioned metal key, and I struggled to get it to work, all the time watching Noah.

And then he looked up, looked right at me, and smiled.

Finally the key turned, and the car leapt into the air. The word 'magnetosphere' lit up on the dashboard and some sort of blue force field beamed into existence, like we were trapped in a giant blue bubble.

I'll ask Johnnie later, I thought, and slammed my foot down. The right pedal shot us forward like a bullet, missing a diving Noah but smashing through the control panel and straight into the side of the space ark. Creatures tumbled out of smashed containers and I yanked the gear stick back. Nothing happened, so I shoved it forward and this time we shot backwards,[24] smacking Nobody to the floor with a satisfying grind of metal on metal. Noah was still crouching low, half hidden and frantically jabbing at his phone.

I soon realized why. Above our heads the space ark was beginning to open. Bright electric blue light danced about, filling the void. And without another thought I pulled back on the steering wheel and we thrust upwards into the light.

In moments we were free, shooting into the black of empty space.

------

24 Who invented gear sticks that way round???!!
See Secret 87: HOW TO DRIVE A CAR WHEN YOU'RE STILL ONLY A KID
J xx

I whooped with joy and shouted so Johnnie could hear me in the boot. 'We're free, Johnster! We're free!'

Then I saw how close we were to the *Red Rover*; it was right ahead, a large red dot nestled among the stars.

'I can see Mum and Dad's rocket!'

'Eliza –' Johnnie's muffled voice came from inside the car boot – 'I've got some bad news. I was trying to make a milkshake, but I just spilled the milk . . .'

Then the engine cut out and something started

flashing yellow on the dashboard.

'Eliza, did you hear me? I just spilled the milk.'

I fiddled with some of the switches, but only managed to turn on the radio. Then another dashboard light came on.

Noah's voice came through on the car radio. 'Did you really think it would be that easy? I've cut the engine and initiated the self-destruct. You've got thirty

. . . no, twenty-nine seconds, you little *gump*.'

I immediately felt myself struggling for breath. My face was hot with fear; we were drifting in black space with low air and a self-destruct device in the boot. We were doomed all over again.

Johnnie's voice came shouting through for a third time.

'Eliza, are you even listening to me? I've spilled my milk on the alpha vampire squid. And it's getting bigger!'

HOW NOT TO CRY OVER SPILLED MILK

So here we are again. It's Day 5 and I'm stuck in a car. And the car is floating in space, a million miles from Earth. I can hear 'Life on Mars?' singing out from one of the speakers.

1. LOW AIR

2. REHYDRATING SQUID

3. BOMB

And my baby brother Johnnie has got it worse. He's trapped in the boot with our dog and a bomb. And he's just spilled his milk on a dehydrated vampire squid that's about to rehydrate and suck away at their faces.

You're probably worried about us. You're probably holding your breath, thinking, *What happens when the air runs out?* And, to be honest, I'd expect to be worried too. But sometimes you just have to learn the lesson life is trying to teach you. Life can be tough; it can throw bombs and zombie parents and vampire squid at you. The other kids might laugh at your hair because it's different; your teacher might go nuts because you were busy thinking of something else. You might even fall down in PE and get stamped on by Sadie Snickpick's brand-new football boots.

But all that really matters is that you don't live your life in fear. Every child is born thinking anything's possible, but sometimes we forget. In that moment, for some reason, I remembered what Dad had said: anything *is* possible when you let go of your fear.

It's all very well realizing this, but when your baby brother is screaming and that scream seems to be muffled by a vampire squid, you don't have much time for planning.

'Johnnie? I'm going to pop the boot.'

Johnnie's screaming stopped abruptly.

'Johnnie? Can you hear me?'

No answer. The dashboard bomb light flashed: **20 SECONDS**.

'I need to tell you, before it's too late. Back on the beach, when I said, "It's so hard to like you" . . . Well, I was wrong to say that. There's so much to like. You're my best friend, Johnnie. Thanks for being my little brother.'

Still no answer. The dashboard bomb light flashed again: **15 SECONDS**.

I popped the boot and Johnnie floated out; he had the bomb in one hand and was fighting off a rapidly rehydrating vampire squid with the other. It was time for me to take a leap. I knew exactly what I had to do to save Johnnie and Myrt. I had to take a leap of faith. A leap of faith in myself.

I opened the car door, ready to push myself out, but my right hand just wouldn't let go of the steering wheel. Johnnie and Myrt were going to die, but I couldn't let go.

Then I heard a voice in my head. I swear it was Dad's voice. 'Elizaroo, you hero, you're the Girl Who Never Gives Up.'

Suddenly my mind was jumping on to the brown sofa as it slid over the cliff, was diving after Johnnie as he sank to the bottom of the ocean, zipping through a rainforest and talking to 691 million people. I was riding a giraffe and firing up a rocket. I *was* the Girl Who Never Gives Up.

And without thinking any further I launched myself into space.

I caught Johnnie in a flash and shoved him back in the direction of the open car door. But not before grabbing both the squid and the bomb. With ten seconds left I jammed the bomb in the squid's chomping mouth, pushing Myrt towards Johnnie and the safety of the front seats. Then I braced my back against the car's rear bumper and had time to aim the squid before the bomb erupted.

HOW TO SURVIVE A BOMB IN SPACE

My plan had been pretty simple. Get Johnnie and Myrt safely in the car. And use the explosive force of the bomb to give us enough thrust to catch up with Mum and Dad in the *Red Rover*. The only problem was that I'd have to use my body to shield them from the full force of the blast.

Heroic? Perhaps.

Brave? Almost certainly.

Utterly stupid? Definitely.

Successful? Totally.

The explosion wasn't huge to be honest. It flared purple-red, like an indoor firework. But I felt myself pinned to the car by the force of it. And nobody could have predicted that the vampire squid's jelly body would be so effective at protecting me and directing the explosion so accurately at Noah's chasing space ark. And no one could have predicted the impact it would have.

Noah's space ark simply vanished. No last words, no bulging eyes, no shaking fist of fury. Just empty space.

I managed to scramble inside the car and between gasps Myrt licked my face in pure joy. Johnnie worked the steering wheel (like any five-year-old

would), but it didn't make any difference. With unerring accuracy my squid-bomb thrust was perfect to a degree. We caught up with the *Red Rover* in minutes and, with the low air light flashing red, joined them with a loud thump.

Johnnie had his to-do list out. It felt like he'd written it a hundred years ago. He handed it to me with a nervous smile.

There was only one thing left to do.

TO-DO LIST
- ~~Locate secret island~~
- ~~Get survival kit~~
- ~~Get pirate ship~~
- ~~Find secret island~~
- ~~Rescue Mum and Dad~~
- Make Mum and Dad want us again

HOW TO MAKE YOUR PARENTS WANT YOU AGAIN

'What if we can't turn Mum and Dad back into normal people?' asked Johnnie, squeezing my hand.

'They were never particularly normal in the first place,' I joked feebly.

Docking seemed to take ages. But when we finally did, and the doors opened to let us enter, we were met by two smiling faces. Mum and Dad. Their eyes were kind, but also sort of glazed over. My heart started beating faster. We were never going to get them back, not properly. Noah had destroyed our mum and dad. He'd destroyed our family. If you ever get the chance to turn your mum and dad into mindless zombie robots, don't. No matter how tempting it is.

Then Myrt growled. It was one of her attack growls, and she leapt at Dad's head.

For a moment I thought he must be wearing orange, but then I saw the truth. Our angry, savage, wonderful dog had a new nemesis. And with champing front teeth, she bit into the robot centipede's tail, tugging it from my dad's skull and down into her mouth. Mum looked blankly on as Myrt did the same to her BIN. And a moment later Myrt was happily crunching by our feet like a dog with two bones.

With the centibots gone Mum and Dad both started to shudder. We looked up at them and waited. I half expected them to blink awake and suddenly be back. But it didn't happen like that.

Mum looked at me, squinting her eyes like I was really blurry or far away. Dad just kept blinking.

'Maybe give them a cuddle?' said Johnnie.

So we did. Johnnie hugged Mum and I hugged Dad. But it was like hugging a tree.

I couldn't look at Johnnie. I couldn't bear to see his little chin wobble, see his face collapse as all the hope drained away. So I just squeezed. I squeezed Dad with every ounce of strength I had. I buried my face in his side and let my brain scream.

How dare they leave us? HOW DARE THEY? So STUPID to get trapped by Noah and his centibots.

I was so angry. All the anger that I'd swallowed down over all those years just seemed to come bubbling up. Anger at Sadie Snickpick and her stupid mean jokes and her fancy shoes. Anger at Mr Murray for making us use a real cricket ball in PE, and Mrs Crosse for making me feel stupid when she was the one who couldn't explain long division properly. Anger at Johnnie for always having to be better than me and most of all anger at Mum for working all the time and telling me I'm brilliant when I'm not, and Dad for stopping playing with me and making me grow up when I wasn't ready to grow up. But most of all anger at me for being so scared of it all. For not making things be different.

Then I bit Dad, hard.

'Owwwh!' It was Dad's normal voice. I looked up, horrified at what I'd just done. 'Eliza, what are you doing? Just give me a minute, will you?'

I looked over at Mum. She was smiling and reaching out with her free hand. 'Hi, little one, are you OK? Don't worry; I think we're back now.'

SIX WEEKS LATER

Six weeks later, we're all safely back on Earth and our parents are almost back to normal.

Life is pretty much the same as it was before.

Sadie Snickpick is still a Butt-Flush Bully.

Mrs Crosse, my maths teacher, still gets cross for no reason.

And my PE teacher is still trying to kill me (I swear it's true).

But somehow things are just different. None of it matters quite so much. We've got our own secret holiday island for one thing. And the publishers of *The Book of Secrets* have agreed to publish our story, which is **<u>AMAZING</u>**.[25]

And I've even stopped worrying about Johnnie being cleverer than me.

We each have our strengths.

JOHNNIE CAN MAKE A WORKING ROCKET OUT OF LEGO.

I CAN TEACH MYRT HOW TO HOLD AN EGG IN HER MOUTH.

WOW!

And we each have our weaknesses.

---

25 It's called *How to Survive Without Grown-Ups*.

And it turns out Mum and Dad don't even care how good we are at stuff. They just want us to be happy.

But the main thing is that we're back together. We're a family again. We're still the Weird Family, but that's always been kind of cool. It's how I like it. If you're weird, stay weird.

For example, only just now, Mum and Dad were tinkering with Noah's car.

When this happened:

The car, Mum, Dad – they all just vanished, instantly replaced by a really old-looking tree.

I looked at Johnnie and he raised his eyebrows.

'Well, I guess they got the time machine working then,' he said. 'I'd better get the chainsaw.' And, with no further explanation, off he went.

EDITOR'S NOTE

Eliza's notebook abruptly finishes at this point. I myself found it at the base of a sawn-down oak tree in her parents' garden five months ago. The tree had come down on the family home, but no member of the family has been seen since.

Despite the continued absence of Eliza Lemon and her family it is to be hoped that they will return to claim their money from the book sales and perhaps recount their latest adventures.

APPENDIX 1

Secret 33: How to Get Your Parents to Do Exactly What You Want

Getting parents to do <u>exactly</u> what you want is easy.

If you really want something, just say: 'But, Daddy, everyone in my class has one and they're laughing at me because I don't have one. And now I have to play on my own at break time.'

If you want to stay up late, just say: 'I'll miss you so much when you're dead, Mummy – can I please have thirty more minutes with you now?'

If you want to play a computer game, just say: 'Ottoline in my class is a year ahead of me in maths because she's allowed to play [insert name of computer game] and it has lots of maths learning on the higher levels. Does that mean she'll be my boss when we grow up?'

ACKNOWLEDGEMENTS

With thanks to two of the **best teachers in the world**, the *real* Mr Murray and the *real* Mrs Crosse (Who is Never Cross!) whose names I stole and are *nothing like* the characters in this book. And also to Eliane, the best cafe in the world, which, by coincidence, is next to Hungerford Bookshop, the best bookshop in the world. And thanks to my first (unpaid) editors, Charlotte, Georgie, Charlie, Isabelle, Eliza and Johnnie for never using the words, 'total rubbish'.

Thanks to Katie, too, for illustrations better and funnier than I ever imagined.

And especial thanks to Becky, Ali, Lowri, David and Jesse for making it all so easy and fun.

And, finally, thanks to Rachel Boden for teasing out the good bits in my first drafts and convincing me that I was onto something.

THE ADVENTURE
ISN'T OVER . . .
JOIN ELIZA AND JOHNNIE
AS THEY DISCOVER:

HOW TO
SURVIVE
TIME
TRAVEL

COMING SPRING 2022